Unintended
Consequences

Unintended Consequences

By
Jim Shevlin

E-BookTime, LLC
Montgomery, Alabama

Unintended Consequences

Copyright © 2016 by Jim Shevlin

All rights reserved. No part of this book may be reproduced or transmitted in any form or by any means, electronic or mechanical, including photocopying, recording, or by any information storage and retrieval system, without permission in writing from the copyright owner.

This is a work of fiction. Names, characters, places and incidents either are the product of the author's imagination or are used fictitiously, and any resemblance to any actual persons, living or dead, events, or locales is entirely coincidental.

ISBN: 978-1-60862-637-3

First Edition
Published February 2016
E-BookTime, LLC
6598 Pumpkin Road
Montgomery, AL 36108
www.e-booktime.com

Dedicated to

The Few. The Proud.

Other Books by Jim Shevlin

A Soldier's Contract, Broken

The Commonwealth Empire

*Government By and For Government
Shall Not Perish From This Earth*

When Freedom and Justice Collide

*Misfortune or Murder?
A Peconic Bay Mystery*

An Act of Wanton Violence

Acknowledgement

I would like to thank the members of the Port Washington, NY detachment of the Marine Corps League for sharing their experiences and encouraging me to create this tale.

Author's Note

Besides the few and the proud, there are other elites who come into our lives, and in my life there exists a small, diverse, and compact group of exceptional men and women.

I would like to cite one such person. I suspect that if I openly identified this person, it might fracture our current friendship. This person shuns any suggestion that its life is unique and extraordinary, but its behavior proves otherwise.

This person reached out a hand in friendship, and that act changed who I am. To this day, I am amazed that this one person could have such a profound effect on my life, and to quote the words from songs, "you set my spirit free," "now I can smile because of you," and "you make me feel brand new."

Despite themselves, circumstances and conduct conspire to make heroes out of otherwise ordinary people.

Most of you are familiar with the words found in John 15:13, "Greater love hath no man than this that a man lay down his life for his friend." Is it a corollary to that thought, no greater friend is that person than the one who saves your life?

I am in awe and overwhelmed knowing that I have a friend who is a hero.

Prologue

When the USS Falcony sailed from Virginia for the Mediterranean Sea, no one aboard the ship expected that the voyage would be anything other than routine, but events ensued that contradicted that perception. A confrontation that occurred would have unintended consequences that neither crew nor passengers could have predicted.

Part One

1

Respect or Lack Thereof

Lance Corporal Jimmy Geracollo was chipping paint on the ship when he heard, "Marine, get off your ass and get back to work."

"That's what I'm doing, my job."

"What did you say to me?"

"I said, I'm doing the job you assigned me to. I'm chipping paint on this old rust bucket."

"How dare you talk to me like that? You are one arrogant Marine. Stand up. I am an officer in the United States Navy, and you will address me as 'sir' when you speak to me. Do you understand?"

"Yes sir."

"Good, now that we understand each other, what do you have to say for yourself?"

"Excuse me, sir but can I speak freely?"

"Go ahead, but keep it respectful."

"Well sir chipping paint is no job for a Marine. It's a job for one of your swabbies because that is what they were trained for. I was trained for fighting anybody who gets in my way on land or at sea."

"You were assigned to this detail by a Marine gunny, and now you are under my command, so you will follow orders whether you like them or not. You don't have a choice."

"Sir, may I continue?"

"Go ahead, but be careful what you say this time."

"The reason I was sitting down is because where the wall and the deck meet, the area is very dark because of the upper deck overhang, so I had to get down low to find out what needed to be chipped. I had a choice of kneeling or sitting, and I decided my ass could take the discomfort better than my knees. That was how I got where you found me."

"Finish the job standing up. No more sitting down."

Feeling that his work ethic was not appreciated, he continued to speak, "Two more things, sir. I don't know about the Navy, but in the Marine Corps respect is earned, and at this point you haven't earned any of my respect. Finally, it's not just me, all Marines are arrogant."

"Stay out of my way or you'll be working in the mess hall tomorrow scrubbing pots and pans."

"Aye, aye sir."

Jimmy went back to scrapping paint. He placed his right hand on the wall and was chipping left to right when his tool ran over a very smooth spot, and in a flash, the tool dug a gash into Jimmy's right hand.

The wound bled freely. Jimmy dropped the tool on the deck, removed his t-shirt, and wrapped it around his injured hand. He moved quickly to sickbay while dripping blood, and by the time he arrived there, his shirt was saturated with his blood.

Nurse Lieutenant JG Nora Pettite reacted quickly when she saw Jimmy's bleeding hand. She gently placed her finger tips on Jimmy's arm and slowly slid her fingers down to his hand and removed the bloody t-shirt. She then cleansed the wound and applied a sterile dressing. She instructed Jimmy to use his left hand on the dressing to stem the blood flow. To reinforce her instruction, she placed her hand over Jimmy's and softly applied pressure.

All the time that Nora was working on Jimmy's wound, he felt something that all men are familiar with, a tingling running down his leg. When Nora saw the familiar starry-eyed flirting look in Jimmy's eyes, she removed her hand from his and called the doctor.

The doctor, Lieutenant Amy Cohalan, inspected the wound and decided sutures were necessary. She sewed up the wound and instructed Nora to apply a clean dressing and secure it. The doctor said to her patient, "Don't get the wound wet. The sutures will dissolve in a week. If you a have any problems, come back and see me. You can return to your unit now. You are finished working for today."

When Jimmy returned below decks to join his fellow Marines, he ran into his good friend, Gunnery Sergeant Vince Ascenzio. Vince took one look a Jimmy and said, "You look like you're walking on a cloud. What's up?"

Jimmy replied with, "I heard that heaven was missing an angel, but I just found her. She's a nurse in sickbay."

"Be careful Marine. She's a naval officer."

"She could be an admiral. I'm going after her. No one can stop a Marine from going where he wants to go."

"Good luck. I hope you enjoy the brig."

Vince never did ask Jimmy about what happened to his hand.

* * * * *

Ensign Richard Settie was making his rounds and was checking to see that every member of his detail was hard at work. He was planning to give special attention to Jimmy Geracollo and thoroughly inspect his work. When he got to Jimmy's station, he was both pissed off and overjoyed to find Jimmy missing. His immediate thought was, "Now I got that lazy Marine bastard. His ass is mine now."

In his haste to leave the area, he almost missed Jimmy's scrapper lying in a dark corner of the deck, but at the last moment he caught sight of the tool. He bent and picked up the object and placed it in his pocket. Excited by the prospect of nailing Jimmy, the ensign failed to notice the dried blood on the blade of the scrapping implement.

Leaving the ship's deck, Settie moved rapidly in the direction of the onboard JAG officer's work station. He found Lieutenant Commander Theresa Scafidi in her cubicle. He knocked on her glass partition and waited for a response. Theresa waved him in, and when he entered, she said, "Pull up a chair. What can I do for you, Ensign?"

"I want to bring charges against Marine Lance Corporal Geracollo. To wit: failure to obey a direct order and abandonment of his post."

"Please explain."

Ensign Settie went on to explain the earlier meeting with Geracollo and that the Marine was missing from his post during his latest inspection.

"Was there anybody in the area that could explain his whereabouts? Maybe he went to the head."

"There was no one else there."

"Did you organize a search for him? Maybe he was injured or unconscious."

"I yelled for him to present himself, but he did not appear, so I came here."

"Okay, I'll look into this and let you know what I find out."

Commander Scafidi checked the ships directory and then dialed the number for Captain Frank Gregory.

When his phone rang, he answered, "Captain Gregory."

"Captain, this is JAG Officer Scafidi. Could you come to my work station? We need to talk."

"What's this about?"

"Lance Corporal Geracollo seems to be absent from his work detail, and Ensign Settie wants a piece of his ass."

"You mean Dickhead Settie?"

"None other," Theresa replied.

"Give me a few minutes to check this out. I'll get to you in the next half hour, okay?"

"I'll see you then."

Captain Gregory went in search of Gunnery Sergeant Vince Ascenzio, and when he found him, he asked, "Gunny, where is Geracollo?"

"I think he's in his rack, sir."

"What's he doing there?"

The gunny went on to explain what happened to Jimmy.

"Come with me," the captain ordered.

Captain Gregory rapped on the glass of the commander's cubicle and waited.

The commander hung up her phone and waved the two Marines into her work space. When they were in front of her, she said, "Take a seat please."

The men sat in folding chairs, and then the commander addressed the captain, "Do we have a problem, or have you solved the mystery of the disappearing Marine?"

Gregory responded, "I'd like to let Gunnery Sergeant Ascenzio explain. Go ahead, Gunny, tell her what happened."

"Ma'am, I was ordered to provide ten Marines for a ship's maintenance detail. Lance Corporal Geracollo was one of the men I sent to Ensign Settie. While chipping paint on the deck, Geracollo's tool slipped and lacerated his right hand. He covered the wound and made his way to sickbay where he was attended to by a nurse, Pettite, and a doctor, Cohalan. The doctor put about a dozen stitches into Geracollo's wound and sent him back to his quarters. I met him at our area and told him to get some rest. I spoke to him later and got the particulars of the accident."

"Commander, I understand that Ensign Softie wants to bring charges against Geracollo. Is that right?"

"Gunnery Sergeant, be careful what you say. It's Ensign Settie to you."

"I apologize ma'am, but I'm a Marine and sometimes I get confused with names."

From the captain, "I think that's enough Gunny. Quit before you're in trouble with the commander."

"Yes sir."

Commander Scafidi continued, "Captain, did the lance corporal or the gunny here notify you of the accident and that the lance corporal was back in his quarters?"

"No ma'am."

"Why not?"

"I think I'll let the gunny answer that question."

"Ma'am, it's like this in the Marine Corps. Marines are always getting injured. It's an occupational hazard. When I saw Geracollo's hand, I figured he was still good to go, and I didn't want to bother the captain with a trivial matter."

"Trivial matter? His right hand is incapacitated because he has a dozen stitches in it. How can he do his job?"

"He's been trained to shoot left-handed."

"Thank you for that Gunny."

"You're welcome ma'am."

The commander continued, "Captain, how did you expect Ensign Settie to learn that the lance corporal left his station for a good reason?"

"I figured he'd get a report from sickbay in the daily bulletin."

"He might not get that report until tomorrow."

"In that case, if he was really concerned, he could have followed the blood drops to the sickbay, and then he would have learned what happened to Lance Corporal Geracollo. Case solved."

Commander Scafidi was getting frustrated with her visitors, so she asked the captain, "Are all Marines as good as you two at creating misdirection and confusion?"

"We all try ma'am."

"I'll contact Ensign Settie and inform him that no charges will be made against Lance Corporal Geracollo. Thanks for coming in. The conversation was very enlightening and informative to say the least. I now have a new understanding of what Marine Corps training does to its members. I think I've had enough of you two for one day, so that's it. Have a nice day."

When the two Marines were at a distance from the commander's work station, Ascenzio said to Gregory, "Sir, I think that went well. Don't you?"

"Much ado about nothing. It happens every day."

"If you don't mind my saying, Captain, Commander Scafidi is hot. I wouldn't mind dirtying up the sheets with her."

"Gunny, watch yourself. It's a violation for enlisted personnel to fraternize with officers. Besides, she's a classy lady and you are a low life male slut. I don't think you stand a chance with her. Remember, if you get caught, I can't help you. You're on your own."

"Sir, do you remember the old saying, 'you can't stop a determined Marine from going where he wants to go'? I'm a Marine, and I never retreat from a challenge. Damn the danger. I have to board her ship before she sails away. Rules are for dogfaces and made to be broken by Marines."

"Vince, we never had this conversation."

2

Command Decision Reaction

When the Marines left Commander Scafidi's cubbyhole, she sat back in her chair, closed her eyes, and thought, "What is it about Marines? They never give you a straight answer to a question; they deflect your attention from the topic at hand; they're deceptive, and yet you get the feeling that they are flirting with you while giving you a hard time by beating around the bush."

She was at a loss to resolve these enigmas but concluded that despite their foibles, they oftentimes come across as being rakish, alluring, mannerly, and romantic. With all these qualities, they can charm the pants off you.

Opening her eyes and returning to reality, Theresa dialed the number of Ensign Settie. When he answered, she instructed him to come to her workplace and added, "We need to resolve the issue of your charges against Lance Corporal Geracollo."

"Thank you, Commander. I'll be there in a few moments."

Fifteen minutes later, Settie was rapping on the glass partition of Theresa's work area.

The commander remained seated and waved to the ensign to enter. When he was standing at attention before her, he spoke, "You wanted to see me."

"At ease, take a seat."

"What have you decided about Geracollo?"

"Slow down, sir. You're getting way ahead of yourself. I'll explain the circumstances surrounding this incident. I just finished a meeting with Captain Gregory and Gunnery Sergeant Ascenzio, and they explained what happened to the lance corporal. Did you know that he injured himself while scrapping paint and took himself to sickbay?"

"No, what did he do, scratch his fat, lazy ass while sitting down on the job?"

Commander Scafidi went on to explain what she learned from her conversation with the two Marines and her decision not to bring charges against the injured lance corporal.

From Settie, "Why do you women naval officers take the side of the macho, egotistical Marines all the time? Are they better looking than sailors, soldiers, and airmen; are they sexier than other men, or better lovers?"

"As a naval officer, I take exception to your tone and accusations. The Marine Corps is an integral part of the Department of the Navy, and as such, I necessarily have to deal with them as part of my assignment.

"I can't speak for all other female military officers or the rest of womankind, but you might have summarized some women's attraction to a Marine. I'll have to consider the possibilities of what you suggest.

"Having said that, I verified that Geracollo injured himself, that it was an accident, and that he was treated in sickbay. I based my decision on those facts and dropped the charges. The case is closed. You are excused Ensign Settie, and don't bring me ridiculous charges like these again."

"Lance Corporal Geracollo should have reported to me that he was going to sickbay."

"What did you expect him to do, confront you with his bleeding hand and ask permission to go to the sickbay while bleeding all over your spiffy uniform?"

"He didn't follow protocol, and he should be punished for it."

"Why do Marines make you feel inferior?"

"I don't feel inferior to them. It's just that their superior attitude is something that is overwhelming to non-marines."

"Maybe you should go to sickbay and see a psychiatrist about your hang ups. This meeting is over. Go!"

"This meeting may be over, but I'm not finished yet with Geracollo."

"Be careful, sir, or you may find yourself going overboard some night in a storm."

Ensign Settie stood, said "ma'am," and left the area.

*****

True to his word, Settie was not finished with Jimmy. He went in search of the third class petty officer who was in charge of the paint scrapping detail, and when he found the man, he asked, "Were all the tools you issued to the men on your detail returned after their shift?"

"No, one scrapper was missing."

"Did each man return the tool you issued him?"

"Yes sir, except the missing one."

"One man went to sickbay. Did anyone turn in his scrapper?"

"No sir."

"Did you search the work area for the scrapper and try to retrieve it?"

"Yes sir."

"Did you find it?"

"No sir, I thought it was lost, washed overboard, or that the man who had it would turn it in later."

"I want you to go below decks to the Marine area and get that scrapper from Lance Corporal Geracollo."

"Hold on, sir, I can't do that."

"Why not?"

"Going down there is way above my pay grade. Do you know what happens to a sailor that invades Marine territory?"

"No, what?"

"He never returns alive."

"I'm ordering you to go down there and get that scrapper. You issued it, and it's your responsibility to get it back."

"I'm not going down there. I'll pay for the scrapper, sir."

"You're not going to pay for it. Go down there and get it."

"I don't think that is a lawful order, and I refuse to obey it, sir."

"I could have you court-martialed for refusing to do as ordered. Now go get the scrapper."

"No sir, I'd rather be in the brig than in the cemetery."

"Are you afraid of the Marines? Don't you know that military rules prohibit them from harming you? They're not a street gang."

"Sir, I've been in fights with street gangs, and the Marines are worse than any street gang in the world. Prohibiting a Marine from doing something doesn't guarantee that he will not do it. I'm not going down there. My mother didn't raise a stupid child."

"You coward! Get out of my way sailor. I'll take care of this myself."

Settie was determined not to be sidetracked by the unconcern of others, so he made an appointment to see the ship's executive officer, Commander Timothy Sampson.

When Settie arrived at the commander's stateroom, he knocked and waited for instructions. A response to his knock came a few seconds later, "Enter."

Ensign Settie entered the room and reported to Commander Sampson.

"What's your problem sailor? Make it quick. I have a ship to run."

"Sir, a Marine aboard this ship has failed to return a piece of government property, and I want a search of his area so the property can be recovered."

"What is this piece of property?"

"A paint scrapper, sir."

"Are you shitting me sailor, a paint scrapper? Excuse me, but how long have you been in the United States Navy?"

"A little less than a year, sir. I graduated from the Naval Academy last May."

"Well, that might help explain some of your ignorance. Let me explain something to you. Both my parents were Marines, and I know from experience that Marines don't go around stealing paint scrappers. If they are going to steal something, it usually will be a weapon that they plan to use on someone. If this Marine has your paint scrapper, I think he plans to scrape your skin off with it.

"You're on a fool's errand, but I'm going to give you the rope to hang yourself. I'm going to kick this down to Lieutenant Commander Scafidi."

Sampson picked up the phone and dialed Scafidi. When she answered, he spoke, "I'm sending Ensign Settie over to see you, and I want you to help him organize a search of the Marine quarters."

"Oh no! Excuse me, sir, I meant to say aye, aye."

"I know what you meant, Commander. It's okay. I feel the same way. Thanks for taking this man off my hands. He's all yours. Good luck with the search."

Sampson hung up the phone and ordered, "Go see Lieutenant Commander Scafidi. She'll help you with the search. I hope you survive this ordeal in one piece and live to tell your children how you escaped death at the hands of an angry Marine. Unless you have a life-threatening situation, don't come back to see me, or you may find yourself run out of the Navy."

Ensign Settie slowly made his way toward Commander Scafidi's post because he was not looking forward to the confrontation and humiliation he knew was coming.

When he arrived at his destination, he found Commander Scafidi standing in her doorway, and she greeted him with, "I was hoping you had the courage not to show up, but I guess a fool and his sanity are soon parted. Get inside and take a seat." She stepped out of the doorway and allowed him to pass through.

When both the naval officers were seated, he addressed her, "You don't have to speak to me that way. I'm an officer and not some deckhand, and I deserve respect from a fellow officer."

"I've given dirty, greasy, sweaty, and asocial deckhands more respect than I'll ever afford you because they have earned my respect by doing their difficult jobs."

"Still and all, I don't have to be subjected to your abuse just because you out rank me."

"What are you going to do about it, bring charges against me like you did Geracollo? Go see Captain Florenze and explain to him that I'm a female chauvinist pig and a loud-mouthed, aggressive, and bossy bitch. Go to see the captain now, and I'll wait here for his call."

"How stupid do you think I am? I'm not going anywhere near Captain Florenze, now or ever."

"That's the first intelligent thing you have said since I met you. Now that we've settled that, let's talk about your search, but before we do that, may I suggest that you drop this vendetta."

"I'm not going to forget it. That enlisted Marine insulted me, and I want him to be punished for his insolence."

"If you want him to pay for his insolence, looking for a paint scrapper is the wrong way to go about it."

"I can't go after him for his insolence. He'll only deny it. It's my word against his, and I can't prove it because there are no witnesses. The search is the only way I can get him."

"This is your last chance to walk away."

"I'm going to see this through to the end."

"It may be your end."

After Settie left her area, Scafidi thought to herself, "I really don't want to get involved in this pissing contest, but I have no choice." Reluctantly and with apprehension, she dialed the number for Marine Captain Frank Gregory.

When he answered with, "Captain Gregory," she responded with, "This is Lieutenant Commander Scafidi again, sir. I'm sorry to bother you, but I need a list of your company's NCOs."

"I can do that for you Commander, but what is this all about if you don't mind my asking?"

"I think we have a property theft aboard the ship, and I need to organize a search party for it. I believe your Marines are best suited to conduct the search."

"I'll send Gunnery Sergeant Ascenzio to you with the list within the hour."

"Thank you. I appreciate your cooperation. If you can accompany the gunny, that might be the appropriate time to apprise you of the situation."

"We'll see you later."

Captain Frank made up the list and then went to find Ascenzio. When he found him, he said, "Come with me Gunny."

"Where are we going to, sir?"

"To see your girlfriend, Lieutenant Commander Scafidi."

"I hope that's a direct order, sir, because I intend to obey it."

"Gunny, stop thinking with your gun."

When the two Marines appeared, Scafidi invited them to take a seat and opened the conversation. "I have a delicate situation that I need to deal with, and I need your help. Ensign Settie has insisted on a search of Lance Corporal Geracollo's belongings for the missing paint scrapper he was issued."

"Oh no, not this bullshit again."

"I'm sorry, Gunny, but I have no choice. I don't want to have a mutiny because of this."

Captain Gregory jumped in, "Gunny, she has no choice, and she's right. We're in the best position to avoid trouble, so we'll do the search."

"Captain, did you bring the list of NCOs?"

Gregory handed her the list, and she scanned it for a few moments and then said, "I need a team of five men to do the search of your area, but to be honest, I don't know who the best men for the job are. Could you pick them?"

"I think I'll let the gunny handle that."

Scafidi handed the list to Ascenzio. Vinny did not bother to look at the list and announced, "I'll take charge of the search, and I'll need Staff Sergeants Stefani and Donnerly, Sergeant Cheetam, and Corporal Welles."

"Thank you, Gunny. I'm relieved, and I owe you one. Can either of you assure me that there won't be any negative reactions, now or later, by your men against the ship's crew?"

Ascenzio responded to the question, "No one will act up if he values his life. Should someone vocally or otherwise resent our intrusion, Staff Sergeant Stefani will personally stifle him. I assure you no one wants to have a confrontation with him. Everyone is scared to death of him. His nickname is The Assassin."

"Captain Gregory, should I oversee the search?"

"I'd advise against it ma'am. I don't want any distractions, and I'm sure you would be a distraction among the men. I'll inform you of the results of the search."

"Thank you, Captain. Now go and make your preparations."

When the pair was outside in the passageway, Gregory said, "Have the NCOs meet in my quarters after chow at nineteen hundred hours so we can discuss the search."

"Yes sir."

The search team met, and the team members were given their assignments. The meeting was over in a few minutes.

The Marines were assembled at 08:00. When Captain Gregory entered the troop area, the first Marine to spot him commanded, "Attention on deck," and the troops responded appropriately.

Then Gregory addressed them, "At ease. Everything in this area will be searched, including equipment, lockers, and sea bag contents. The object of the search is to locate a piece of naval equipment, namely a paint scrapper. If anyone has any information concerning said item, step forward now and we can avoid a lot of hassle."

No one moved, so Gregory continued, "Gunny, proceed with the search. Report to me in my cabin when you are finished."

The gunny called the troops to attention, and when Gregory left, he commanded, "At ease. Each man will empty the contents of his locker and sea bag and place all items neatly on his bunk and remain at ease next to his bunk.

"Corporal Welles, inspect the head, showers, and stationary equipment. Sergeant Cheetam, inspect all lockers to be sure they are completely empty. Staff Sergeants Stefani and Donnerly, inspect each bunk thoroughly for the missing object."

During the inspection, Donnerly exclaimed, "Whoa, what is this, Marine?"

Private Claude Jayson answered, "It's a paint brush, Staff Sergeant."

"What's it doing here?"

"I use it to wipe the dust off my weapon, Staff Sergeant."

"Very thoughtful of you, Jayson."

The search continued for a little over an hour, and between one hundred and fifty and two hundred bunks were examined. After the search was concluded, each of the five inspectors reported his findings to the gunny. Ascenzio announced to the troops, "Stow your gear," then he headed for Captain Gregory's quarters.

"What did you find"?

"There was a thorough search, but no paint scrapper was found."

"That's a relief."

Captain Gregory made his way through the passage ways of the ship until he arrived at the cubicle of Commander Scafidi. Theresa was surprised to see Frank in her doorway, but she recovered quickly and invited him in and then asked, "Is it good news or bad news?"

"That depends on how you look at it. We didn't find the paint scrapper; good news for Geracollo and bad news for Settie."

"Thank you. I appreciate the way you and the gunny handled the entire affair."

"You're welcome, ma'am. I'll leave now."

Lieutenant Commander Scafidi ordered Ensign Settie to report to her office, and when he arrived and knocked on her door, she responded, "Enter."

He stood at attention before her and waited for her next command. After looking at some paperwork on her desk, she spoke, "The search came up empty. Your charges against Lance Corporal Geracollo are dismissed. Get out of my office and never ever bother me again."

A smile crossed Settie's face, and he said, "Yes ma'am," and then left.

When he was back in his quarters, Settie said to himself, "That went well." The smile returned to his face because he planned to use the blood-stained scrapper at some time in the future.

Part Two

3

Redirection

The Marines had use of the ship's deck for two hours each day. On the morning of March 20, 2003, Captain Gregory led his men in a series of calisthenics, followed by push-ups, sit-ups, and pull-ups. A two-mile run around the deck finished the physical training for the morning.

As the troops rested and rehydrated themselves, Captain Gregory waved Gunnery Sergeant Ascenzio to his side. "Gunny, have the men form a semi-circle on the deck and remain seated. I want to address them."

Ascenzio passed Gregory's order to the other NCOs, and a few minutes later the company commander stepped in front of the Marines and spoke, "Marines, some of you may have heard some scuttlebutt about what happened yesterday. This is what happened. Last night at 21:34 Washington time, a coalition led by the United States began bombing Baghdad.

"Our orders have been changed. Instead of resupplying in Rota tomorrow and then moving on for some fun in the sun, sand, and surf, we will disembark there. From Rota, we will travel north overland to a combined Spanish US airbase at Moron and be flown to Kuwait, where we will join the war effort. Get your equipment in order, get some rest, and be prepared to move when the ship docks. Gunny, get the men ready. Training is over."

As the men began to move, Private Claude Jayson said to Jimmy, "What the fuck is the captain talking about? Where the fuck is Baghdad?"

"It's in Iraq."

"I thought we were going to Spain. Where the hell are Rota and Moron?"

"They're in Spain."

"Good, I can't wait to get to the whorehouses there."

"For a minute I thought the captain of the ship got us lost on the way. I'm glad Captain Gregory knows where he's going. Sailors don't know which way is up, stupid bastards."

As Gregory walked away from his men, Ascenzio howled, "You heard what the captain said, move it."

While the Marines were making their way below decks, the gunny grabbed hold of Jimmy and pulled him aside. "Geracollo, the rules say we can't take an injured man with us, so if you don't want to go back to the States on this ship, you better get rid of those stitches. Get your ass to sickbay and get them removed."

"Gunny, I'm not going to miss this rodeo. The stitches are supposed to fall out by themselves when my hand is healed. My hand will be okay in a couple of days. If they're not out by the time we get to Barcelona, I'll take them out myself if I have to."

"Use your head. Go see that nurse you have goo-goo eyes for and have her give you some TLC."

Jimmy made his way to sickbay and was delighted to see that Nurse Pettite was on duty. He entered the sickbay and asked, "Lieutenant, could you help me?"

"Oh, it's you. I didn't think I'd ever see you again. What do you need help with?"

"I was hoping I would see you again, but to be honest, that is not the only reason I'm here. I need these stitches out of my hand."

"They should fall out by themselves in time."

"I know that, but I may not have the time to wait."

"Why?"

"My company is getting off this ship tomorrow or the next day."

"Where are you going?"

"We are going to Rota as planned, but we're getting off there and going to Moron."

"I heard the war started in Iraq. Is that where the Marines are going?"

"Probably."

She held his injured hand in hers for much longer than was necessary to inspect the wound and then started to remove his stitches.

Jimmy's back was to the sickbay entranceway, so he did not see Ensign Settie enter the room, but he heard him say, "Hi Nora, how are you? Change of plans. We're dumping the Marines at Rota. How about we go ashore and have a night on the town?"

The nurse did not answer as the ensign moved close to her, but when he was standing next to her, he exclaimed, "What are you doing here Lance Corporal?"

With a big grin on his face, Jimmy responded, "The nurse is treating my wound."

Nora was aware of the condescension of many Marines toward Navy men. This disdain often manifested itself in rejoinders like, "sailors are the Marine Corps' seagoing, taxi drivers."

When leaving a ship, the Marines often comment to the nearest seaman, "thanks for the ride sailor."

To sum up, the Marines never thought of themselves as the stepsons of the Navy, but rather as the big brothers in the family protecting their younger, less aggressive, seagoing siblings.

In order to prevent an outburst, Nurse Pettite, in a commanding voice, warned, "Ensign, you are not allowed in this room while I'm treating a patient. Please leave."

Settie left the room, but there was no smile on his face like the one he had when he left Commander Scafidi. He was angry because a "nothing" Marine had embarrassed him again. He vowed to avenge the insult.

Jimmy said to Nora, "Thanks for throwing him out. If you didn't do it, I was going to kick his ass through the doorway."

"And then you would have ended up in the brig. I don't know how your being in jail solves your problem. The egotism of men is now the scourge of the human race."

"We can't help ourselves. It must be part of our gene makeup. Marines don't take shit from nobody."

When Nora finished removing the sutures, she swabbed the scar with iodine to blend the light skin color with the tan of his hand, and then cupped the injured hand between her hands and gently caressed it. After some long moments, she released the hand and said, "Off you go."

"I'd like to make the same proposal that the ensign offered you earlier. How about you and I go out on the town when we reach Rota."

"There are several reasons why I should emphatically say no to your offer. If we went out together, it might prove to be very dangerous for both of us. You know about the rules against fraternization between officers and enlisted men. A meeting for the two of us is almost impossible anyway. Neither of us knows what will happen when this ship docks at our destination."

"Since you didn't say no, I gather that you're not opposed to my offer, so I'll leave it on the table for another time in the future."

"You never give up do you?"

"Surrender is never an acceptable alternative for a Marine."

"When this ship gets back to the States, I'm scheduled for shore duty. If fate, destiny, or God deigns to send you home safely, look me up."

Nora felt she was losing control of her emotions as tears welled up in her eyes. In order to bring the situation back on an even keel, she simply uttered, "Stay safe, and now please go."

"I won't forget you."

The day after Captain Gregory addressed his Marines, the USS Falcony docked in Rota, and the company prepared to disembark. On Gunny Ascenzio's order, each man hoisted his sea bag onto his right shoulder and followed Gregory down the gangplank.

Ensign Settie was stationed to the right and slightly above the gangplank and was supervising the disembarkation. As each enlisted Marine passed the naval officer, he extended his right middle finger.

Settie was overwhelmed with anger at the sight of enlisted men demonstrating such arrogance toward an officer and to him personally, but he knew there was nothing he could do about it except to tolerate the audacious behavior. He could not complain to higher-ups because he could not identify any individual as the troops passed by quickly. He also understood that none of his superiors would believe that an entire company of Marines had the cajones to act with a singular purpose.

To further anger him, he noticed that many of the sailors working on deck were showing grins and smiles in agreement with their fellow enlistees and would be of no help with the presentation of his argument.

The low ranking naval officer had yet to learn that discipline, like respect, was earned by leadership and not by issuing orders.

To the left of the departing Marines and at some distance away from the gangplank, stood Lieutenant JG Nora Pettite and Lieutenant Commander Theresa Scafidi. Their presence went unobserved by both the ensign and the Marines.

Each woman was vainly attempting to catch sight of a particular Marine that they each held a special affection for, but the search was fruitless, because by design, the members of a military unit looked so similar, in uniform, to each other that individuals could rarely be recognized. The purpose of the design was to make each member of the group interchangeable with any other member of the group.

The women were spectators as opposed to participants in the activity on the deck and were relegated to the role of bystanders who could only stand, watch, wait, and pray for the safe return of the men who had aroused those dormant stirrings in their hearts.

As the Marines made their way north, Nora moved around the sickbay making a list of the medical supplies that would be needed to restock the shelves of the sickbay. The job was boring, and she was filled with a feeling of ennui.

As he passed the sickbay, Ensign Settie saw that Nora was working alone, so he popped into the room and announced, "Nora, a group of the junior officers is going ashore tonight for a get-together and a few drinks. I'm inviting you to join us. What do you say?"

Nora was caught off guard and hesitated for several moments before answering. Several thoughts flashed through her mind in a few seconds. She was lonely and depressed, she was sure she would never see the Marine with the wounded hand again in this lifetime, and she needed to escape the confines of the ship, so she replied, "Okay, I'll join the crowd."

It cannot be explained why men and women interpret the same event in different ways. The nurse was in a state of forlornness and only wanted a change in her current condition and environment, while the ensign was confident that he had secured the first of many dates. He was looking forward to playing doctor with Nora, after office hours, in the future. Nora was hoping that at some time, in the future, she would be able to engage in mattress gymnastics with a lance corporal.

The trip from Rota to Moron was approximately seventy-five miles, and the caravan of Marines arrived at its destination in time for lunch, so instead of eating MREs, they dined on salad, steak, potatoes, and vegetables, accompanied with a dessert of apple pie ala mode. The Marines feasted like it was their last meal, but the gunny warned his men, "Don't eat like pigs. If you puke it up later, you're going to clean it up and be on guard duty all night."

Private Claude Jayson leaned into his friend, Private Wally Covence, and jawed, "Holy shit, Wally, look at those Air Force guys. They have go boxes of food, and look at that fat fuck over there. He's leaving with a cone of ice cream topped with sprinkles. These guys are all fucking fags."

4

Over There

The Marines spent that night at Moron trying to digest both the lunch and the dinner provided by the Air Force.

For breakfast, most of the Marines could only ingest coffee and dry toast, but they were saddened by the fact that they were forgoing eggs, bacon, sausage, French toast, pancakes, SOS, and sweet buns. None of the men upchucked during the night, and every man wanted to avoid using the barf bag on the plane flight to Kuwait.

Captain Gregory and his Marines landed at Ali Al Salem air base, which was jointly operated by the Kuwaiti Air Force and the U S Air Force. Near the airbase was a former Marine base. It was a remnant of the Gulf War twelve years earlier. The base was an updated tent city.

The Marines were invited to join the airmen of both countries for their meals in the ultra-modern chow hall. The Marines were too late for the luncheon hours, but they enjoyed a sumptuous feast in the evening.

After breakfast the next morning, Private Jayson grabbed hold of Jimmy Geracollo, and as was his custom, he began bitching, "Can you believe this bullshit. These flyboys are stationed in a shithole in the middle of the ass end of the world and are eating like kings. To top it off, our fucking government is feeding the Arabs better than it feeds its own Marines. When I get home, I'm gonna find the recruiter who convinced me to sign up for this crap and kick his ass up and down the street til he can't walk anymore.

"The thing that's really going to piss me off is when I find out that even the Army dogs are eating better than me. I can't take much more of this bullshit."

Jimmy came back with, "I hope I'm not near you when you find out that all military people are not treated equally. Later."

"Wait a minute," Claude responsed to Jimmy's dismissal, because in any conversation, he always wanted to have the last word. He continued, "Last night I nearly froze my ass off, and now I'm sweating like I ran a marathon. What's up with that?"

"You're in a desert, and that's the way the temperature goes; up during the day and down at night. Get used to it."

"I'm beginning to hate that recruiter more and more. That bastard."

Part Three

5

Road to Baghdad

The ground forces of Iraqi Freedom launched their attack on 20 March, 2003 from a point close to the Iraq-Kuwait border. The march to Baghdad was a two pronged assault with the forces advancing in parallel lines.

Captain Gregory's Marines were camped about thirty-nine miles from the Iraq border inside Kuwait, and a couple of days after the war started, in the early morning, the Marines rode into Iraqi territory on LAV-25s. These light armored vehicles were Marine infantry standard rides. Included in the group were LAV-ATs (anti-tank).

Gregory's orders were plain and simple. The Marine company was to crisscross the initial assault lines for a length of five miles in each direction, searching for anything unusual.

Everybody in the command structure expected the search to be fruitless, but it looked good on paper, as if the Marine company was actually a part of the war effort, and it could keep the unit busy until it caught up to the main force a few days later.

In mid-morning as the Marines approached a large dune at the eastern end of the five-mile limit of the search area, a forward scout vehicle returned from patrol, and a scout signaled Gregory to halt forward movement. The captain gave the order, and all vehicles stopped in place.

Captain Gregory dismounted his vehicle and moved in the direction of the scout, who reported, "Sir, there is a concrete shack about two hundred yards out. I think it's a communication outpost because of the tall antenna. It's too far from our guys, and I think the Iraqis forgot about it. It looks like a six man detail."

The captain gave the signal to mount up and move forward. As the unit crested the dune, an Iraqi soldier who was having a smoke in the shack's doorway shouted to his comrades and pointed to the top of the dune. The smoker did not run into the shack to send a warning. He ran to the back of the outpost and hopped into the truck parked there. The mechanic working on the truck heard the warning, slammed the hood closed, and then jumped into the driver's seat and started the truck.

The other four men were sitting in a circle around the sides of a latrine they had recently dug and were dumping their excrement. When the warning came, two of the Iraqi soldiers stood up, pulled up their pants, and headed for the truck. As the pair jumped into the truck, the driver took off.

For the other two dumpers, things did not go well. In a state of confusion, they both fell backward into the latrine with their weapons. The first soldier scrambled out of the pit and was weaponless. He pulled up his trousers and ran over a nearby dune.

The second man crawled out of the toilet, dropped his weapon, struggled to pull up his pants with one hand, and raised his other arm in a half surrender motion while walking toward the Marines.

Captain Gregory took command of the situation immediately. Through the vehicles' intercom network, he ordered, "Donnerly, turn the building into rubble. Cheetam, don't let the truck get away. Blast it."

Donnerly did not move his vehicle. He took time to sight his target and then fired the anti-tank gun. In the blink of an eye, the shack exploded and pieces of concrete rained down on the sand.

Sergeant Cheetam flew after the fleeing truck, firing the 50 caliber machine gun while closing the gap. When Cheetam was fifty yards behind the Iraqi vehicle, it stopped. The truck was punctured with bullet holes. There was no activity from the truck. The sergeant assumed all of the enemy soldiers were dead, but he was not one to leave an assignment unfinished or take chances, so he fired the anti-tank weapon, and the truck with its occupants exploded in flames. The burning fuel soaked into the sand, and the fires stopped. The only thing that remained was heat and smoke.

Staff Sergeant Stefani was the ranking man in the trailing vehicle, and he heard Gunny Ascenzio order him, "Stay with the prisoner."

Corporal Welles was with Ascenzio and asked the gunny, "Should I go after the guy who ran away?"

"Don't bother. He's not going anywhere. Without a weapon and no water, he'll be dead before evening prayers."

A shot rang out, and Ascenzio turned toward the last vehicle. He started to walk in the direction of the men grouped around that vehicle, and when he was next to them, he asked, "What just happened?"

No one answered his question, but as he was walking away from the group, he heard, "We didn't hear anything, Gunny. We were all taking a piss."

As Ascenzio neared Stefani, he saw that the Iraqi prisoner had died from a bullet hole in his head. The gunny casually asked, "Why?"

"Gunny, I had no choice. He kept jabbering, and I couldn't understand a word he said. I told him a hundred times to stop, but he kept yakking, and then he started crying like he was a baby and wanted his momma. He smelled worse than a cesspool. What the hell do these people eat? I felt sorry for him. I took mercy on him, so I shot him to get him out of his misery. Look at him now. He's at peace. All his worries are over."

When the gunny approached Captain Gregory, he said, "We have a situation."

The captain asked, "What happened over there, another accidental weapon discharge?"

"No sir." The gunny went on to explain what happened with Stefani and then asked, "Is Stefani in trouble?"

The captain did not hesitate, "Our mission is to report anything unusual, and I don't see anything unusual about some dead sand monkeys. I'm sure we'll see more of them before we're finished."

As the captain was moving toward his vehicle, he ordered, "Let's move out Gunny."

6

Gunny Ascenzio

Gunnery Sergeant Vince Ascenzio was born to his parents, Margaret (nee) White and Tony, in Brooklyn, New York on November 22, 1972.

His childhood was a challenge to his parents because Vince had a penchant for asocial behavior that often bordered on criminal activity. He was a precocious child, but not in the sense that most parents hope for. He had above average intelligence but never demonstrated excellence in reading, mathematics, science, music, or the arts.

Vince, by choice or chance, managed to keep his intellectual advantages in the recesses for most of his life. That is not to say that he never had moments of brilliance. Those moments of exceptional mental ability, unfortunately, were few and far between, and the most notable ones were not socially acceptable.

Another form of Vince's precociousness was the early onset of puberty. He was well fed at home, and that, along with a regimen of physical activity, helped develop a big, tall, muscular, and handsome young man. When Vince's young, immature male friend saw the evidence of his male prowess, they agreed that Vince was "The Man."

Vince's stature did not go unnoticed by his female peers, who were also developing their own obvious credentials.

He no longer needed to chase after the young women and flirt with them for a date. The damsels swarmed around him and declared in no uncertain terms that they wanted to sample his assets. Vince found it difficult to deny these flattering invitations, so he mostly succumbed to their wishes.

In elementary school, Vince did not apply himself to mastering the three R's, but instead applied his skills to becoming the class clown or class disruptor. Whenever a teacher asked a pivotal question during a critical lesson, Vince would raise his hand, and when he was called upon to answer, he would give an absurd response and the class would erupt in laughter. The teachers never gave up on Vince because they all hoped that one day he would give an enlightened response. That day never came.

At one time in the New York City public schools, certain students were programmed into classes labeled CRMD (Class of Retarded Mental Development). Had that option been available when Vince was a student, he most certainly would have been seated in the first row, first seat of the class.

Because of social promotion, Vince was spared the embarrassment of repeating any grades. As he prepared for his high school career, Vince for once demonstrated a flash of genius when he took and passed an entrance examination for a specialized high school.

Everyone hoped that this would be a major turning point in Vince's education, and possibly his life, but alas, it was not to be. During his first term of the accelerated curriculum, Vince found himself surrounded by and overshadowed by classmates who thought an education was a goal worth pursuing. By the beginning of the second term of his freshman year, Vince found himself in a new high school.

Vince was transferred to a school not noted for its academic achievements, Franklin K Lane HS in Brooklyn. The actual location of the school is interesting. It is situated on Jamaica Avenue adjacent to an elevated railway. It lies on the Kings County (Brooklyn) Queens County border in an area known as Cypress Hills, which most people believe is part of Queens County. Truth be told, the line separating the counties actually divides the school in half.

I only mention this geographic anomaly because it seems that the school authorities were guided by fate and reassigned a student with uncoupled educational goals to a bisected educational institution.

We all know the quote attributed to Jesus and later used by Lincoln, "a house divided against cannot stand." The same may be true of schools. Franklin K Lane closed in 2006.

Vince, in all likelihood, would have been granted either a Certificate of Attendance (a citation indicating that one had actually attended high school) or a General Diploma, but in its wisdom, the New York City Board of Education changed the qualifications for graduation to a single academic diploma.

In the latter months of his senior year, Vince made a life-changing decision. It was at a time when the final list of graduates had not yet been promulgated, but it seemed apparent to most, including Vince, that his name would be absent from the list, so he did what many young men did with few options available to them; he dropped out of school and joined the Marine Corps.

On his last night as a Brooklyn teenager before reporting to boot camp, Vince gave his high school ring to an enthusiastic young female friend that he was attached to in the back seat of his best friend's Chevy. To this day, he cannot remember the young lady's name.

On the day before he left for Parris Island, his friends peppered him with questions of why he joined the Marine Corps. Do you want to be one of the elite? Do you want to defend your country? Do you think your uniform will get you more girls? How much do they pay you?

Vince answered some of the questions and fended off others with shrugs, laughs, and expletives. His last words to his friends were, "I want to kill people that I don't like, and the Marines are the best killers in the world."

Vince was a tough teenager, and in boot camp he found out that he was tougher than he thought he was. He excelled at physical training and tolerated the physical and verbal abuse that was heaped upon him to the edge of his restraint. I will say more about a particular boot camp experience Vince endured in a later chapter.

After Parris Island, he moved north to Camp Lejeune for more advanced and comprehensive training. To Vince's and his instructors' surprise and amazement, he took to weaponry like an alcoholic to booze. Whether with a rifle or sidearm, no target was a challenge to him, regardless of the distance.

Instructors often used Vince to demonstrate proper shooting techniques to the other trainees, and he spent extra hours on the firing range tutoring his lesser skilled comrades so they could get qualifying scores.

Some thought of him as a throwback to the Wild West frontier and referred to him as the Brooklyn Cowboy. Others suspected that he was a New York gangster with real life shooting experience in the shadows of organized crime and joined the Corps to escape the long arm of the law. Vince never tried to dispel any of these impressions.

A few months after Vince's eighteenth birthday, POTUS (President of the United States) gave orders to start the first Gulf War, Operation Desert Storm. The war started with aerial and naval bombardments on 17 January, 1991. A ground assault began on 24 February, 1991.

During the ground attack, Vince was a liberated warrior, and the Brooklyn gangster unleashed his own Mid East crime spree. He dared the enemy and death to slay him, but neither succeeded. By the time the battle ended one hundred hours later, Private Ascenzio was Lance Corporal Ascenzio.

Either by force or choice, Vince earned a GED (General Education Diploma), and armed with this document, his rise through the ranks kept a steady pace as he travelled around the globe from base to base.

Lance Corporal Ascenzio was probably ignorant of the quote by the Greek philosopher Heraclitus, "No man ever steps into the same river twice."

As he prepared to leave the battlefield, Vince could not have possibly known that twelve years later he would step foot in the same desert.

Part Four

7

Warfare

"Old men declare war. But it is youth that must fight and die."
                                               Herbert Hoover

On 22 March Captain Gregory's Marines caught up with the main force. Earlier in the day, there was a major tank battle between the coalition forces and Iraqi forces on the western side of Basra. Gregory's unit was not involved in the battle or the cleanup in its aftermath, but as they passed through the area, the men realized that the battle must have been fierce, with heavy casualties on both sides in men and machines.

After observing the burning death traps and the dead who had tried to escape the inferno, Private Jayson commented, "Poor bastards, it must have been like going to hell while you were still alive."

The unit continued its march north toward Baghdad, and on 3/23 joined other Marine forces and engaged in the battle at An Nasiriya. Two days later, the Marines had control of the area and confiscated weapons, caches, protective gear against chemical weapons, and an older model T-55 Russian tank. All of this equipment was found hidden in the city's hospital.

Not one to let an opportunity for fun pass him by, Lance Corporal Geracollo seized the moment. He found the object of his interest, the tank, in the large basement warehouse of the hospital. Although all of the instrument markings and instructions were either in Arabic or Cyrillic Russian, Jimmy was not daunted by the task at hand, starting the vehicle. He had the utmost confidence in his ability to achieve success.

Unbeknown to others, Jimmy's teenage years were filled with experiences of relocating the vehicles of others without the benefit of keys. The gods of good fortune favored Jimmy that day. He found a stock of vehicle batteries, hooked them up in series, and with a grin on his face from ear to ear, he started the monster.

To establish himself as a New York celebrity, Jimmy prepared for his grand entrance. As he drove the T-55 onto the city streets of An Nasiriya dressed in a standard white anti contamination suit with a gas mask covering his face, he looked like the Pillsbury Dough Boy in a futuristic sci-fi movie.

As Jimmy patrolled the city, both the local inhabitants and his comrades cheered him on.

The lance corporal's antics were observed by Captain Gregory, and he decided he would have to deal with the situation, so he stepped in front of the tank as Jimmy halted the vehicle. "What do you think you are doing, Geracollo?"

"I'm having fun. I thought I would lead a parade around the city to show these people who's the boss."

"I think these people have had enough of bosses over the centuries. We're just the latest, and they'll be happy when we leave."

"Captain, you sure know how to put a damper on a party."

"I'll make you a deal. You can drive that piece of crap to Baghdad, but if you break down or run out of gas on the way, you walk the rest of the way."

"Aw shit, sir, that deal is like buying an old broken down TV set for a price higher than a brand new one. No deal. I'm out."

"Good decision Marine. Sometimes you amaze me. You're smarter than you look."

Jimmy parked the tank beneath the hospital. His chance for fame and renown on an Iraqi stage had been rent asunder by a Marine Corps officer who had no sense of humor.

8

Lance Corporal Geracollo

Marie (nee Aldofino) and Antonio Geracollo welcomed their son, James, to this world on July 27, 1985. His fighting weight at birth was eight and a half pounds. This was probably an omen of his physique as an adult.

What he did not know during his developing years and would not learn until he was in Marine Corps boot camp was that Vince Ascenzio was a cousin in the third degree.

Although the Geracollos of Manhattan's Lower East Side and the Ascenzios of Brooklyn had met at family gatherings, neither Vince nor Jimmy had any recollection of ever meeting each other.

Jimmy's favorite sports as a kid were football and boxing. He spent many hours playing football on the green fields of the city's parks and on the concrete of the city's streets, without the benefit of protective equipment. These activities would take a toll on his physical and mental development in later years.

Boxing was a skill that Jimmy thrived on. He challenged an ever increasing number of bigger boys to boxing matches of three rounds. Winner got a Pepsi; loser paid.

Jimmy took enjoyment in the physical contact that went with these sports and absorbed much pain and punishment that was a part of these activities without complaint. His guiding motto was, "No pain, No gain." For the most part, he gave more than he received in the way of suffering. At the end of each encounter, whether on the field or in the street, win or lose, he was content to know that he never backed off.

Jimmy aka Duke was the leader of his gang, and the gang members held him in high esteem because he had a reputation as an accomplished leader and street fighter. The gang prided themselves as the defenders of the less fortunate who were often accosted by neighborhood bullies.

The physical skills that Jimmy had developed would later help him earn the title United States Marine.

Like many youngsters from the lower east side of Manhattan, Jimmy had to endure the trials, tribulations, and rigors of attending a New York City public school while attempting to gain an education.

He was not the most disciplined student in class, but neither was he the worst. On a scale of 1 to 10, one being the worst disciplined student and 10 the most disciplined student, Jimmy's average score was 4 or 5. There was a very small minority of teachers who rated him a passable 6. This group claimed that he could be controlled if you showed him a modicum of respect.

Jimmy believed that respect by one's peers was the highest honor a man could achieve. He had no respect for anyone who had a lordly attitude and treated those who they felt were inferior to them with contempt. This attitude toward others was why Jimmy and Ensign Settie had their differences aboard the USS Falcony. It was obvious to those who knew both men that they were polar opposites, and those in the know would bet the farm that their difference would never be resolved.

Jimmy was able to grasp the rudiments of reading, writing and arithmetic, and he retained a smattering of history, geography, science, and the penal code.

As an older teenager, he was awestruck by the concepts and principles of Philosophy, Ethics, and Morality.

Jimmy was convinced that every successful person needed to develop a personal philosophy that would explain who he was and how he would interact with society. The cornerstone of his philosophy was that he needed to very strongly believe in something that mattered to him. He also believed that expressing a philosophy would endear him to those more learned than himself.

One day as he lunched with his confessor, the man asked, "Jimmy, what do you believe in?"

Jimmy answered without hesitation, "I believe we should have another round of Jameson 12 year old."

The priest responded with, "Jimmy, I don't think you understand the basic concept," but the man did not try to explain Jimmy's misunderstanding. In the spirit of friendship, he continued, "That's a splendid idea and our best possible course of action."

During his seventeenth year, Jimmy was faced with the same quandary that his third cousin, Vince Ascenzio, had encountered: what to do about his future.

The die had been cast, and Duke knew that he would not stroll across the graduation stage, so he pondered the alternatives of continued education, the job market, or the military.

The option of continued education was slimmer than none. No institution of higher learning in the United States would open its doors to him without a diploma, and he had no funds for vocational training.

His prospects for gainful employment in the job market were only slightly better than a college career because he had no saleable skills other than gang leader and brawler. Some young men in Jimmy's predicament were fortunate to have a rabbi who could obtain a union apprenticeship for them. But Jimmy had no such champion.

Jimmy thought about joining the Army, but he discarded the idea because he was averse to discipline, taking orders, and to the idea of taking long marches. Excessive walking did not appeal to him as a worthwhile form of exercise.

He thought that the Navy was a viable alternative. Jimmy envisioned himself seeing the world while sailing the seven seas, eating three squares a day, and getting paid for it. An added benefit was that women engaged in the oldest profession in the world had a strong attraction for sailors. The only downside was swabbing decks and chipping paint on the ships. He held onto the idea of life as a seafarer until that option no longer was viable.

Fate has a way of stepping into our lives and making life-changing decisions for us in ways that we don't always appreciate. Such was the case for Duke when he created a scenario that would take decision making out of his hand.

It seems that for some unexplained reason Jimmy decided to take possession of a law enforcement patrol vehicle. The result of his joyride was an arrest when his so called friends threw him under the bus, backed up over him, and told the authorities that he was the sole perpetrator of the theft.

Like all accused, Jimmy was entitled to a day in court. A transcript of the court proceedings indicated a verbal exchange between Jimmy and the judge. It went something like this. The judge, "James Geracollo, you are accused of stealing city property, namely a police car. How do you plead?"

"Yeah, I did it."

"I'll take that as a guilty plea. What possessed you do something so foolish?"

"I thought it would be fun. I'm a fun loving guy. My father's taxes paid for that cop car, so I felt I was entitled to a free ride."

"The tax system doesn't work like that, as you now know. You made a very poor decision, and now it's my turn to make a wise one. Since this is your first reportable serious offense, I'm going to give you a choice. You can go to jail, or you can walk across the street to see a recruiter and join the Marine Corps. It's your decision."

"Can I join the Navy?"

"The modern day Navy runs on nuclear power and electronics. Do you know anything about those topics?"

"I don't remember learning anything about those two things in school."

"I thought not. Your place on the learning curve indicates that you are best suited for the Marine Corps or jail. It's either one or the other."

"Judge, that's like picking between worse and worser. My friends told me to pick jail, but since my friends got me into this mess in the first place, I'll take the Marines."

"Good, I'm sure you chose wisely. Will the court officer please escort this young man across the street to the Marine recruiter?"

"Thanks for nothing Judge."

"You're welcome. Some day you will thank me for giving you this opportunity. I'm sure the Marine Corps will keep you out of further trouble with the justice system."

If only the judge had gazed into a crystal ball and seen Jimmy's future, his last words might have been different.

9

Boot Camp

Along with other young men from the northeast, Jimmy was heading for Parris Island, South Carolina. The future Marines boarded a train at Grand Central Station in New York City and travelled toward their destination.

In the evening, the train stopped in Yancy, South Carolina and discharged the enlistee passengers. The group moved to and slept in some makeshift barracks overnight. In the morning, the group boarded busses for the final leg of the journey to Parris Island.

The bus stopped in an open area and began the ejection of its cargo. As the men came off the bus, they were greeted with a litany of orders issued by a DI (Drill Instructor). "Line up on the side of the bus; drop your bag in front of you; move your ass over there stupid; and you pieces of shit are the dumbest bunch of recruits I have ever met, God help me. What's the Marine Corps coming to?"

When the men were assembled in proper formation, the DI knocked twice on the door of the bus, and the driver moved his vehicle away.

Without preamble, the DI launched into his monologue, "I'm your drill instructor, Staff Sergeant Jankow, and my job is to make Marines out of you losers. When you speak to me, you will start by addressing me as Staff Sergeant. If you address me as Sergeant or Sarge, you will regret it for the rest of your life. Never speak to me unless I give you permission. If you open your mouth at the wrong time, you'll be sucking your meals through a straw. Follow every command I give you to the letter, no exceptions. Don't fuck with me. If you do, I'll fuck you up so bad you'll wish you were never born. Some of you sacks of shit were bad asses back home, but you're not home anymore. You're in my home now, and I'm the baddest ass you're ever gonna meet. If you put your hand on me, you'll never use that hand again. You'll have to jerk off with the one you have left.

"I'm going to march you over to the chow hall. Stay in line. Don't step on your dick or the guys behind you will walk right over you. Don't drop your bag. If you drop it, keep going. It's lost. You'll never see it again. Don't eat like pigs. If I see you doing that, I'll push your face into the slop and make you suck it up like the cocksucker you are."

In the mess hall, the trainees, including Jimmy, loaded their trays with food because most of them had nothing to eat in the last twenty-four hours. When the last man was seated, Jankow gave permission for his group to start eating. After five minutes, he ordered, "Put your forks down, pick up your tray, and walk over to the garbage cans and clean your tray into the garbage. Put the empty tray neatly in the bin and place the utensils in the basket. Then line up outside. Now."

Some of the men tried to eat their food with their hands while waiting in line for their turn at the garbage pail. When the men were lined up outside the mess hall, Jankow howled, "You pigs who ate with your hands, wipe them clean on your pants. The Marine Corps prides itself on cleanliness."

The next stop was the barbershop. Some barbers had a sense of humor and asked their customers, "How would you like it?" Some recruits gave instructions, but others said nothing because they knew what was coming. All military people know what happened. The barbers with instructions and smiles joined their coworkers in the shearing. Each man received exactly the same haircut. It was the beginning of interchangeable parts.

Haircuts were followed by the issuance of uniforms and equipment, all of which was stuffed into a duffle bag. As the men exited the building, they milled around in small circles chatting while waiting for the last man to come out. When Jimmy came out, he dropped his duffle bag on the ground and sat on it.

When the staff sergeant followed the last man out and saw Jimmy sitting on his duffle bag, he slowly walked over to Jimmy and asked in a friendly voice, "What's your name, Sitting Bull?"

"James Geracollo." Jimmy started to say more, but he was cut off.

"Whoa, whoa, whoa stop talking. When you address me you start with Staff Sergeant. I told you that before. You must be as stupid as you look. Why is your ass sitting on Marine Corps property? Don't you respect Marine Corps property?"

"Staff Sergeant, I'm sitting on Marine Corps property because my ass is tired."

"How could you be tired you lazy fuck? You haven't done anything all day. Pick up your duffle bag. We're going to the barracks."

By now all the recruits were gathered around the conversation waiting to see what happened next.

Jimmy replied, "I can't pick it up. It's too heavy, and I'm too tired."

"Can't. Nobody in the Marine Corps ever says can't. This isn't the Army, Navy, or Air Force."

Jankow moved closer to Jimmy and said in a calmer voice, "Maybe I've been asking too much of you today, Geracollo, so I'll tell you what I'll do for you. With your permission, I'll carry your bag for you, but you must agree to walk yourself to the barracks. Is that okay with you?"

"Staff Sergeant, that would be great. Thank you. If you carry my bag, I think I can make it to the barracks if it's not too far away."

Jankow picked up Jimmy's duffle bag, organized the men, and then led them to the barracks. Jimmy made the trip to the barracks successfully, but everyone knew that from that moment forward Jimmy's life would be unbearable in boot camp.

The DI placed Jimmy's duffle bag on his bunk and directed the recruits to do the same. When each man was standing at attention in front of his bunk, the DI spoke again, "This isn't summer camp for a bunch of mamma's boys. This is Marine Corps boot camp. If you are going to survive here you have to do what you're told to do when you're told to do it. No questions. No can'ts. No tiredness. No nothing except yes I can, Staff Sergeant. Geracollo, step forward."

Jimmy stepped forward.

"At ease. Your training starts now. Geracollo, where are you from?"

"New York."

"Look at him, he thinks he's back in New York and can sit down anytime he's tired. He thinks he's a tough guy and he can do anything he wants anytime and anywhere he wants, but he's not going to pull any of that bullshit here. His attitude sucks, and I think he's a punk and a hoodlum from the gutters of the city's streets who was pussy whipped by his slut girlfriend. Let's see how tough he is. Drop down and give me twenty."

What we know that Jankow didn't know was that Jimmy was in good physical condition. Jimmy dropped to the floor and did the twenty push-ups with ease. When he started to stand, Jankow shouted, "Stay down and give me another twenty!"

Jimmy did the additional twenty and then rested in the upright prone position and waited to do twenty more, but the command never came.

Jankow was pissed, but he knew he might embarrass himself if he kept asking for twenty and Jimmy did a hundred push-ups, so he ordered, "Stand up. You look like you're trying to bang the cracks in the floorboards."

Jimmy stood up, and the DI moved down the line berating every man he faced.

The staff sergeant vowed to break Jimmy and make him quit. There came a day when he thought he would achieve his goal. He was moving down the line of men in the barracks debasing each one in turn. When he came to Jimmy, he asked, "What part of New York do you come from?"

"Staff Sergeant, Manhattan."

"Manhattan's a big place. Do you live on the upper east side with the rich people?"

"Staff Sergeant, no. I live on the lower east side."

"I thought so. A ghetto. A slum area."

Jimmy didn't answer. It was a statement, not a question.

"What does your father do for a living?"

"He's a carpenter, but he's unemployed right now."

"So he stays at home and drinks all day. He's a drunk."

Jimmy flinched but did not respond. It was another statement.

The DI continued, "I guess your mother has to support the family. Where does she do her hooking, down in Chinatown or on the docks with the tourists and the sailors? How much does she get for a blow job?"

Jimmy couldn't take anymore. He slammed his right fist into the left temple of Jankow. The blow stunned the DI, and he staggered back a few steps, but he did not fall. Jankow recovered and then stormed back at Jimmy and rained blows down on him.

Jimmy put up his arms to defend himself, but he did not fight back. He had made his point. He did not back down from his tormentor. He was never one to tolerate bullshit from an asshole, and this DI was the biggest and most degenerate asshole he ever met. He knew his Marine Corps career was over. He knew he would be on his way home the next day. He also knew that he could have killed this low life scum, but he did not want to spend the rest of his life in jail. What an irony, he had joined the Marines to stay out of jail, but now it might be the Marines who led him to jail.

Jimmy walked himself to the medical facility, and when Doctor Amanda Camisa saw him, she asked, "What happened to you?"

"I walked into a door."

"That must have been a moving door. It walked all over you."

The doctor treated Jimmy for cuts and contusions after taking x rays that proved negative. She gave Jimmy several chemical ice packs and told him to place the packs on his head, arms, and chest. She advised rest, but both doctor and patient knew that might not be possible.

While Jimmy was being treated, Gunny Sergeant Ascenzio called Staff Sergeant Jankow into his office. When Jankow arrived, he asked, "What's up, Gunny?"

The gunny said, "Let's go outside. I want to talk to you."

When the two were outside the barracks, the gunny asked, "Why did you do that to Geracollo?"

"I never liked that son of a bitch from the first time I saw him. I always wanted to get rid of him, and today was my chance. He hit me first. He's done."

"I think you went too far."

"Too far? Nothing is too far. You know the deal, Gunny. We have to break these guys down to the lowest form of life and then build them back up again until they take all kinds of shit without question. We want them to become robot killing machines.

"Don't you remember the drill? Steers and Queers from Texas. Blonde surfer dudes from California who are gay faggots. Kentucky hillbillies who marry their sisters and first cousins. The gangsters from New York. The druggies from South Florida. If they can't take it, they don't belong here. Are you getting soft on these pussies, Gunny?"

As the DI went through his diatribe mentioning what was wrong with the inhabitants of every state in the country, Gunny Ascenzio had a recollection of an experience he had in Marine boot camp. Like Jimmy, the DI had profaned Vince's mother, and like Jimmy, he punched the DI in the head. The DI reacted by breaking Vince's jaw with a counter punch.

When Vince reported for medical attention years earlier, the doctor asked the standard question, "What happened to you?" And Vince gave the standard reply, "I walked into a door."

Vince's DI was a lot smarter than Jankow, and he realized that Vince had the making of a good Marine, so he stopped harassing him, and Vince successfully completed his training.

"Jankow, I don't think you understand your role here. We're not making robots out of humans. We're here to train these boys to become men and Marines, the best fighting force in the world."

"The training has been the same for over two hundred years, and I'm not going to change it now, and you can't make me."

"I'm ordering you to stop with the mothers."

"Mothers are fair game."

Vince realized that his words had failed to educate the man, so he said, "Maybe this will change your mind."

Vince decided to take a time-proven course of action that often resulted in mind changing. He punched the staff sergeant in the head. The man did not go down, and a brawl broke out. After both men were battered, Jankow said, "Enough."

The gunny said, "Go get yourself fixed up."

Jankow made his way to the medical facility, and when Doctor Camisa saw him, she asked a question that she already knew the answer to, "What happened to you?"

"I walked into a door."

The doctor treated the patient and then sent him on his way. When the man left the area, she turned to her nurse and commented, "I wonder if we're going to have another outbreak of the door virus?"

Gunny Ascenzio reported to the company commander, who asked, "Were you sparring without head gear?"

"No sir. It was a misunderstanding."

"Should I ask what it was all about?"

"I'd rather you didn't, sir."

"Okay, why are you here?"

"Jankow has to go."

"Should I ask why?"

"I'd rather you didn't, sir."

"He's gone."

When Jimmy returned to the barracks, he was told to report to Gunny Ascenzio.

Jimmy knocked on the gunny's door and was told to enter.

"You wanted to see me, Gunny?"

"You look like shit. Can you explain what happened?"

"When DI Jankow asked me how much my mother charged for a blow job, I couldn't take his bullshit anymore, so I hit him. I look like shit because he beat the hell out of me."

"Why didn't you fight back?"

"I knew I was wrong, and I was hoping he would forget about it if I let him beat me up. I'm sure he'll report me, and I'll be thrown out of the Marine Corps. I was wrong to hit him."

"The damage was already done, so you were wrong not to defend yourself. Marines always attack, not go on the defensive. You were right to throw that punch, and you should have kept punching until you sent him to the hospital."

"Then I'd be going to jail instead of home."

"Jankow's going. You're staying."

"Thanks, Gunny."

"Don't thank me yet. The bullshit starts again tomorrow morning. Staff Sergeant Kennedy will be the new DI. I suggest that you don't take a swing at him. If you do, he'll put you in the hospital."

Under the tutelage of the staff sergeant and the gunny, Jimmy excelled in all things physical, weapons, and taking orders. During the training period, Jimmy and Vince learned that they were distantly related, and within the protocols allowed by Marine Corps boot camp, they became friendly.

At the end of boot camp, Ascenzio opined to Kennedy, "Geracollo has come a long way. He has the makings of a great Marine."

Jimmy left Parris Island and travelled to Camp Lejeune in North Carolina to complete his training. Private Geracollo, as he did after his dustup in boot camp, excelled in all phases of the program.

After he completed schooling at Lejeune, it was time for his next assignment. Marine Corps postings on the surface may appear random, but those making the postings argue that there is a sound military foundation for their decisions.

Many educated and experienced observers of the military have come to the conclusion that all military decisions are guided by the gods of discord, farce, and absurdity. This conclusion may explain Jimmy's next posting to the Brooklyn Navy Yard in New York. After months of Marine training, he would be an MP (Military Police) guarding Navy property.

For those of you who are not aware of it, the Marine Corps is a part of the Navy Department. Some historians think that the Marine Corps is the unwanted offspring of an illicit affair between consenting Navy admirals. Because of the long running turf war and a long list of differences in critical thinking between sailors and Marines, the Navy decided to permit the troublesome prodigal sons to partially separate from the Navy family and create a family of relatives under the patriarchal leadership of the Navy.

All of this confusion could have been avoided if the early naval commanders had called their security force sea soldiers instead of

Marines. Once the Marines had an identity, all bets were off, and what resulted was The Few, The Proud, The Marine Corps.

Jimmy's initial reaction to his posting was one of disappointment, but the more he thought about it, he began to see the advantages of this assignment. He would be near home. A trip over the Brooklyn Bridge would deliver him to his parents and friends, and it was better than a posting to some shithole in Asia.

When Jimmy was on station in Brooklyn, some of his former asocial attitudes began to surface. His first run in with the Navy brass was when he and his fellow Marine MP buddy, Ed, purloined a ship's compass. The purpose of the theft was to sell the compass to the highest bidder or the local pawnshop.

The selling of swag does not always go as planned. When the theft was uncovered, Jimmy, not one to be caught with his hand in the cookie jar, was prepared for this reversal of fortune. Jimmy had learned as a gang leader in Lower Manhattan that when caught red handed with the loot, one should have an alibi.

Jimmy and Ed claimed that they had taken the compass for the protection of Navy property, as was there duty, to prevent its theft by unsavory characters in the surrounding crime ridden neighborhoods. The compass was restored to its rightful place on the ship. There were no charges filed.

The next episode that brought Jimmy and his cohort to the attention of the authorities was when they discharged their weapons. The pair were target shooting at the bottles they placed, at varying distances, on the tops of the bulkhead pilings.

Newly appointed NYPD (New York Police Department) officer, Louis Wurth, and his training officer, Dave Santo, heard the gunshots and drove onto the pier to investigate the gunfire.

Training Officer Santo decided to let his student handle the situation and make arrests if necessary. The officer approached the pair of MPs and asked, "What are you shooting at?"

Jimmy was prepared to answer, and he did, "We weren't shooting. Guys in a boat shot at us. I think they were Mafia."

"Why did you draw your weapons?"

"We were going to protect ourselves if they came closer and shot at us again."

"Why are there shards of glass on the pilings?"

"They must have been lousy shots and hit the lights on the pilings."

"Holster your weapons." It was done.

Louis knew he would get a scathing rebuke from his Marine father if he made an arrest, so he went over to the police car and asked his trainer, "Can we go?"

Santo replied, "Good idea. Let's go get coffee."

There was no police report filed.

The next incident was the straw that broke the Navy's back. The naval officer on duty found Jimmy on guard duty on a very cold, winter night, very drunk and without any pants. The officer relieved him of duty and replaced him. The officer went to the guardhouse and sent an email to the duty officer at Camp Lejeune. He requested that the Marine Corps recall Jimmy and send orders to that effect.

The Marine officer replied, "Will comply. Faxed orders will follow."

The next day Jimmy was on a bus for the return trip to Camp Lejeune. There was no report filed.

Were the gods of discord at it again? Was Jimmy's first posting a forewarning of things to come?

Part Five

10

Moving Forward

The city of Najaf sits astride important highways leading to Baghdad. On March 24 Apache helicopters carried out a mission against the Iraqi Republican Guard.

Constant attacks by Iraqi forces against American supply lines forced the ground attackers to slow their advance for several days in order to secure their supply areas and capture the city.

Captain Gregory's group was charged with the security of the resupply convoys to Najaf. The next part of the story might come under the heading, "Military Intelligence, An Oxymoron."

This is what Gregory understood the game plan to be. The Army supply convoys would travel at the highest speed possible under existing road conditions toward their destinations, with the Marines following the convoy to provide protection. If the convoy was attacked, the vehicles still mobile would continue forward with the greatest possible haste toward the destination. The Marines would deal with the attackers.

If a convoy vehicle was disabled for any reason, whether it was from an enemy attack, mechanical failure, or driver ineptitude, the vehicles behind the disabled one would drive around it and continue with the rest of the convoy. The Marines were responsible for dealing with the aftermath.

When enemy forces attacked a convoy, the Marines would engage the force in a firefight and either repel the force, or kill the attackers quickly. If neither of these two options were successful, the engagement would continue until reinforcements arrived and the enemy was defeated. Any enemy action that resulted in injury or death to a coalition soldier would also be dealt with by the security force.

In the case of mechanical defect, all efforts would be made to get the vehicle moving under its own power or by towing. If the vehicle remained immobile, it was destroyed along with its cargo.

When the failure was due to human ineptitude, Captain Gregory had the authority to make any decision necessary to rectify the situation. In most cases, he simply replaced the Army dog with a qualified Marine driver.

On April 2 Captain Gregory and his men were again providing convoy security. In most cases, the convoys sped along the left side or middle of the road to avoid IEDs (Improvised Explosive Devices) that were usually placed on the right side of the road where most traffic flowed.

On this particular day, when the lead vehicle rounded a curve, the driver saw a string of pickup trucks heading toward him in the left lane. He was forced to move right as the enemy knew he would. The pickup trucks were driven by insurgents whose job was to force the convoy to the right.

The enemy plan worked. The lead vehicle hit an IED. The truck exploded and took a couple of pickup trucks with it. The convoy was stalled, and it soon came under rifle fire. The second driver drove into the left lane and pushed the pickup trucks over to the side of the road and continued forward. The rest of the convoy followed the new lead vehicle with increasing speed.

When the lead vehicle exploded, the security force knew what to do. It had been well trained. The men jumped off their vehicles and took cover behind a roadside embankment and then returned fire. The enemy was firing down on the Americans from a tree-lined crest above them.

Like many well-travelled roads in Iraq, the top of the roadside embankment provided a slit trench latrine and a hand wash trough.

At this point I have to digress. Most Muslim Iraqis are guided by Sharia law, which prescribes certain penalties for certain crimes. As an example, if a man is found guilty of theft, the penalty is severance of his right hand. I only mention this because if you

Unintended Consequences

happen to visit friends in the Mideast and a former thief offers to shake your hand with his left hand, you should refuse the greeting.

You might ask why? Because most men in these countries wipe themselves with the left hand and then wash that hand in the communal trough. If you accept that hand and then eat with your fingers or hands, as many do in those cultures, in all likelihood you will suffer from a severe case of Typhoid fever.

Back to the battle. Aside from the rifle fire, the Iraqis started to lob motor shells and RPGs (Rocket Propelled Grenades) on the Americans. Most of the shells fell short or long of the troops, but some of them took a path into the latrine. When these bombs exploded, everyone in the vicinity was showered with urine and excrement.

Captain Gregory was not one to tolerate a shit storm lightly, so he got on the radio and called for an artillery barrage. A few minutes after he had given the position of the enemy, 8-inch howitzer shells rained down on the enemy position. The trees on the crest were torn into firewood. When the barrage ended, there was no movement on the crest. The enemy was either dead or the more self-reliant ones had retreated.

Staff Sergeant Stefani assigned men to collect the body parts of the truck driver and his passenger. The driver's remains were placed in a body bag, but the men couldn't find any body parts of the passenger. The passenger, he or she, was reduced by the explosion and ensuing heat to a pulpy, jellylike mass of protoplasm. A pail full of the mass was collected. A DNA test would identify the passenger.

The pail, along with the body bag, was placed on the floor of a security vehicle. Former riders in that vehicle sought transportation elsewhere, but everyone could not be accommodated. The hearse vehicle carried the remaining privates and lower ranking NCOs.

Privates Jayson and Covence were seated next to Lance Corporal Geracollo, and the three started to engage in gallows humor.

Private Jayson started with, "I wonder what they do with all these body parts in the morgue? They have to make sure that the boot sizes match. Could you imagine the lawsuits if they put two right hands or two left feet or a long and a short arm in a coffin and someone opened the casket at a wake? Those people aren't stupid if they can't find matching parts. They just say the missing parts were blown away in the explosion."

Lance Corporal Geracollo added, "I wonder how they package that blob of goo? Do they put it in an old mustard jar, a plastic bag, or a coffee can? I hope they put instructions on the coffin; do not open under penalty of law."

Private Nicky B ended the conversation with, "You guys are sick bastards. Shut up."

The conversation ended, and the men fell silent as they looked at the remains of the dead soldiers as thoughts that came to all combat veterans entered their minds; thoughts of their own immortality. This thought process usually ended with the understanding that if I survive today, I will die tomorrow, because war is a useless political tool, and at the end of the shooting, there will be no winners; only a long list of the maimed and the dead.

When the company returned to camp, each man stripped down to his birthday suit and dropped his shit-covered clothing into a pile. No one knew or cared whether the reeking pile of excrement would be burned or cleaned. What they all knew was that they would have clean clothes in the morning so that they could go back out on patrol. The only question that remained was would they have to pay out of their own pockets for the new uniforms. It would be a moot point if they died tomorrow.

On April 4 the city of Najaf was in American hands. Captain Gregory's company was not there for the celebration. It had moved on to its next assignment.

11

Al Kut

By April 3 Gregory's company had joined the 1st Marine Division on the outskirts of Al Kut. Warnings were broadcast to the Iraqi forces that they must surrender by a certain time. When the Iraqis did not surrender by the deadline, the US forces began an assault on the city.

In the beginning, the assault troops met little resistance, but when the troops were very close to their objective, Iraqi soldiers and irregulars opened fire with small arms and RPGs. The Americans, not wanting to get involved in a close-quarters city battle, remained outside the city while returning fire. Air and missile strikes were launched against the city, destroying much enemy equipment and killing many of the defenders.

When the American attackers were pinned down by Iraqi fire from a well-defended enemy bunker, the US forces responded with heavy machine gun fire and tank fired shells. After a few hours of this offensive, most of the Iraqi bunker defenders had been killed, injured, or captured.

What happened next was totally unexpected and another example of battlefield stupidity. In a futile last ditch attempt to repel the enemy invaders, the remaining Iraqi soldiers charged the American tanks.

You don't have to be a student of war to know what happened next. The chargers were cut down like weeds to the last man by tank fire, small arms, and machine gun fire.

The 1st Marine Division advanced to capture the city and the bridges of Al Kut.

Staff Sergeant Donnerly said to his buddy, Staff Sergeant Stefani, after the slaughter of the charging Iraqi soldiers, "Those stupid bastards must have thought they were descendants of the men at the Charge of the Light Brigade or Pickett's Charge. I wonder if they would have fared better if they rode into battle on camels."

Stefani responded to his friend, "Camels or no camels, it wouldn't have made any difference. They would have all been dead in any case. Look at the bright side, we don't have to clean up stinking dead camels, but if we did, we could sell the dead camels to the local population for dinner tonight and the rest of the month.

"The towel-heads have only one goal, get to paradise. I guess this was a quick way to get these guys there. I'm glad we were able to arrange passage for them. If I lived in this shithole, I'd look forward to dying in battle too."

Donnerly shook his head in agreement and offered, "The train to paradise is going to be very crowded tonight. I wonder what it's like thinking from the day you are born that you wish and hope that you would die; if not today, then tomorrow."

Stefani closed the conversation with, "You must be some kind of bullshit philosopher. If you ever get out of this dung heap alive, you can write a book about your experiences in this crap hole. Why don't you title the book, *Iraq, Home of the Camel Humpers?*"

Al Kut was the last stop for these Marines before attacking Baghdad.

12

Baghdad

Captain Gregory's Marines were in their vehicles travelling toward Baghdad behind the Marine Corps 2nd Tank Battalion on April 4. The battalion's mission that day was to attack a division of the Iraqi Republican Guard on the outskirts of Baghdad. When the column was a few kilometers from its objective, it missed a turn and entered the heavily defended town of Tuwayhah.

The main road in town was blockaded with old buses, trucks, and a variety of old vehicles. Every building on the road was defended by groups of snipers. The tanks travelled a short distance down the road without any problem. The commander of the lead tank was scanning both sides of the road from an open hatch when the enemy opened fire.

A grenade from an RPG hit the turret hatch and bounced off it into the tank and exploded, killing the commander, cannon loader, and machine gunner. When Captain Gregory's executive officer, First Lieutenant Stan Darby, saw that the lead tank was ineffective, he leaped from his vehicle, mounted the tank, and took command of it. Sergeant Koster followed Darby into the tank and became the cannon loader and machine gunner. Darby got his tank moving and led the battalion through the town, destroying the enemy as he went.

A fierce battle continued through the morning and into late afternoon, but by the end of the day, the enemy had been subdued. After the tank battle, Gregory's men went through the town cleaning out the remainder of the defenders. Among the dead, they found not only Iraqi Republican Guard soldiers, but also Syrians, Egyptians, Lebanese, and Yemeni volunteers from terrorist Islamic Jihad organizations.

After the town was secured, the Marines found massive amounts of rifles, RPGs, and small arms. There were enough arms and ammunition in the town to re-arm another Iraqi division.

Several Marines were killed, many were wounded, and one tank was lost. Unfortunately, the tank lost was the one commanded by Lieutenant Darby. In the last hour of the battle, Darby's tank hit a roadside bomb that disabled the tank, immobilized it, and set it on fire. As the crew attempted to escape the tank, they were cut down by enemy rifle fire. First Lieutenant Darby and Sergeant Koster were awarded Silver Stars posthumously for their daring, valor, and gallantry that day.

The next day, Gregory's company entered a small village just inside the city limits of Baghdad. The mission that day was to clear the village of Iraqi soldiers, terrorist, insurgents, and Saddam Hussein sympathizers so that the larger following allied forces could enter Baghdad properly without being harassed or slowed down.

The Marines would go house to house clearing them of any potential threats. The town was almost completely cleared when Nicky Basasasvilli, aka Nicky B, because no one could pronounce his family name, entered a low, small, one story house with only one window. The inside of the building was very dark because the one window allowed only limited light. As Nicky started to pull back a curtain covering the entrance to a small room, he heard a dog bark behind him.

He turned quickly in the direction of the bark and spotted the dog and an old man standing in a dark corner. The man was holding his thumb on a plunger. Nicky fired his weapon at the man, but he was a split second too late. The man had pushed the plunger down just before Nicky fired at him. As the man was falling, the mud brick wall behind Nicky exploded outward and the resulting vacuum pulled Nicky and the dog out of the building. Nicky was partially covered with the wall rubble and was semi-conscious. The Marines heard the explosion and looked around for the cause of it when a dog started a constant barking that led Nicky's buddies to him. The still barking dog was standing next to Nicky when help arrived. One Marine placed the dog off to the side while others cleared the rubble around Nicky. Nicky, in his semi-conscious state, asked, "What happened?"

Gunny Ascenzio answered, "You're okay, and we're going to get you out of here."

A medic checked Nicky and announced, "He'll be alright. His helmet and his flak jacket saved him from serious injury. He has a lot of deep bruises, but he'll be good to go in a few days."

Nicky B was loaded on a stretcher and placed on the floor of a truck. As the group started to drive away from the village, Nicky asked, "Where's the dog?"

Jimmy Geracollo answered, "He's okay, and he didn't get hurt. Don't worry about him."

From Nicky, "Get the dog."

Jimmy came back with, "It's too late, and we're moving out. He'll find a new home when things settle down."

Gunny Ascenzio looked out the back of the truck and saw the dog running after the truck. The gunny was about to do what he knew he wasn't authorized to do, but he was going to do it anyway. His decision was based on the old adage that it is better to apologize for a decision after the fact than it is to ask for permission before the act, so he ordered the driver, "Stop the truck."

The driver stopped the vehicle. Vince jumped out the back of the truck and picked up the dog. Vince got back in the truck and put the dog on Nicky's chest and ordered, "Move out."

Nicky clutched the dog to his chest and fell asleep. The dog stayed on Nicky's chest for the trip back to camp.

At the camp, Gunny Ascenzio told Nicky B, "Go see the doctor and have him check you out. I want to know when you'll be ready for some more action."

Jimmy Geracollo agreed to watch the dog while Nicky was with the doctor. The doctor checked Nicky from head to toe and took some x-rays. When the doctor completed his examination, Nicky asked, "What do you think Doctor?"

"I think you are a very lucky young man; no broken bones and no damages to your ligaments and tendons. You're going to have some pain and soreness for about a week or two. I'll give you a script for the pain and a note to your commander stating that you'll be inactive for a while." The doctor did as he said he would and then said to Nicky, "You're good to go."

"Thanks Doctor. I hope I don't need to see you again in the future."

"Go with God."

Nicky returned to his area and gave the doctor's note to Vince Ascenzio, who read the note and said to Nicky, "I'll take care of this. You're gonna be stuck here for the next several days."

When Nicky returned to his quarters, he found Jimmy Geracollo washing the dog. Private Jayson was nearby and piped up with, "That's a scruffy looking dog you've got there, Nicky B. It's probably covered with lice, fleas, bugs, and Iraqi shit. Jimmy's wasting his time trying to clean up that mutt. You should take him outside and shoot him."

From Nicky B, "You should talk. You're more scruffy than the dog you unkempt, sloppy bastard, Claude. If anyone hurts my dog, I'll kill them, including you."

Jimmy added, "You better not let the Iraqi mess cooks see him or he'll be on the dinner menu tomorrow night."

Nicky responded to Jimmy's remark, "If that happens, I'll blow up the mess hall. Pass the word around if anything happens to this dog, something worse will happen to the culprit that caused her harm."

Claude tried to show off his command of the English language by commenting, "You dummy, Nicky B. You just called him a her."

With a smile on his face, Nicky turned to face Claude and said, "You're the only dummy here." Nicky went on to explain himself. "The dog slept next to me on my cot last night, and when she rolled over this morning, I saw that he was a she."

Jimmy inquired, "Have you given her a name yet?"

"Yes."

Claude asked, "Did you give her a nice girlie name for Christ's sake?"

"Yes."

Claude was getting frustrated, so he blurted out, "Well, what the fuck is her name?"

"Lola."

13

Lola

While Captain Gregory's Marines went out each day to engage in the battle of Baghdad, Nicky B spent his time training Lola. He taught her to respond to all the ordinary commands used by all dog owners. He ran into some stumbling blocks when he gave his commands in English, because Lola had been trained in Iraqi Arabic.

When Lola didn't understand a command, she had the habit of sitting down with a quizzical look on her face. At first Nicky was frustrated when Lola didn't respond, but he soon understood it was a language problem, which he resolved by demonstrating what he meant. For example, when he said "Go," he would start walking forward with the dog walking beside him, and when he said "Stop," he would stop moving and hold the dog beside him in place. They practiced "go" and "stop" many times until Lola had it down pat. He would give the commands "go" and "stop," and when he wanted Lola to return to him, he would back up while clapping his hands. Lola understood the command and would return to his side and sit down.

Another command Nicky used on a regular basis was "Go to place," and Lola would go sit on her mat next to her master's bed. Lola was a quick learner and soon learned to ignore spoken commands given in her native tongue and learned to react to English as a second language.

Each day, Nicky took Lola to different groups of Marines. He wanted her to recognize the different speech patterns of Marines from different geographic regions of America and the smell of US Marines. When a body breeze blew past Lola's nose, she could tell whether it originated with an Iraqi or an American.

When Lola and Nicky went on the house calls, she always walked beside him and never let him out of her sight. When Nicky stopped to chat, she sat beside him. They had developed an unbreakable bond. On many occasions, Lola sat in the middle of a circle composed of Marines, and as the group chatted, the men would pet Lola and play with her. She felt very comfortable in the presence of Marines, and these sessions brought a sense of contentment to both man and animal.

One day while Nicky and Lola strolled around the camp, a Marine asked Nicky, "What's the dog's name?"

"Her name is Lola."

"Why did you name her Lola?"

The question made Nicky reflect on his decision, so he explained it this way, "When I was a boy, I spent my summers from the time I was eight until I was twelve with my older sister, Laura, on my grandfather's dairy farm. Grandpa Tom's farm was in upstate Oneonta, New York. My grandfather had a dog named Lola. Lola and I spent every day working together on the farm and taking long walks in the countryside. She slept next to my bed every night. I will always remember those days as the best part of my life. This dog is a lot like grandpa's Lola, and she reminds me of my happy youth, so she's a Lola too."

The listener remained silent for a long moment and then responded, "That's a great story, and I wish I had a childhood experience like that. I'm glad Lola makes you happy, but don't get too attached to her."

"Why do you say that?"

"Simple. When you rotate out, you can't take her with you. She's an Iraqi dog, so she stays in Iraq."

Nicky had never thought that far in the future, knowing that he might not have a future. Going home was something fighting men rarely thought about because it was a dream that might never be realized, and when you were in a shithole like Iraq, it would interfere with you doing your job. Taking steps that might keep you safe might also get you and others killed. At that moment, Nicky vowed that he would not leave Lola behind, now or at any time in the future.

Part Six

14

Victory?

About the time Nicky B was ready for full duty, the United States declared victory in Iraq on April 14, 2003.

When word of the victory declaration spread among Nicky's buddies, Private Jayson, while roaring with laughter, exclaimed, "What the hell are the generals smoking? It must be some good shit. If we won the war, why are these towel-heads still shooting at us?"

Gunny Ascenzio responded to Jayson, "I guess Saddam Hussein forgot to pass the victory announcement to his troops while he was racing out of town."

Jimmy Geracollo added, "These sand monkeys are just using us for target practice, and from what I've seen, they're gonna need a lot of practice if they expect to win this game. The Iraqi soldiers are great at losing yardage, getting sacked, and punting, but they suck at getting first downs and scoring."

Captain Gregory overheard the conversation and decided to add his two cents. "My high school rifle team could probably outshoot these guys."

Gregory added a warning to his men, "It's never a good idea to take any enemy too lightly. That attitude might get you killed."

It is interesting to note that while Gregory's Marines were discussing the absurdity of the victory declaration, they were in the midst, with other Marine units, in the battle for Tikrit. The Marines entered the city on April 13 and battled in the last center of Saddam loyalists. It wasn't until two days later on the 15th, the day after the victory announcement, that the city was captured.

The American forces had bypassed a lot of villages and towns in the race to Baghdad, and the military leadership decided to scour these villages and towns to make sure there were no small strongholds left in the country.

Captain Gregory's company was one of several units assigned to the cleanup campaign that would last for the next several months. Another paradox of the Iraq war occurred on May 1, 2003, when President Bush flew onto the deck of USS Abraham Lincoln and gave his infamous speech about the war before a banner that proclaimed, "Mission Accomplished."

At this point, I think its best that I refrain from citing any of the quotes made by the troops about the President's speech. I leave it to the reader's imagination to guess what the quotes sounded like.

Early each morning, the Marines set out to clear a suspected area. Lola always accompanied Nicky's platoon. Lola had been trained to locate roadside bombs and sniff out Iraqis inhabitants inside buildings. She would move into a village about fifty yards ahead of the platoon and search both sides of the road for bombs. If she found none, she would move to inspecting the buildings. She would start at the first building at the top of the road, and if she sensed no one inside, she would move to the next building. If she was convinced that the building was occupied, she would sit down next to it, and those buildings would be searched first. Lola's scouting helped the Marines avoid ambushes within the occupied buildings and saved many of the Marines from injury or death.

When a town or village was cleared, the Marines would return to their camp located a few miles away from the Baghdad International Airport. On several occasions, Captain Gregory would receive orders to make arrangements for pickups at the airport. The trips were for the collection of food, ammunition, needed supplies, government officials, congressmen, or other high ranking VIPs.

The airport was often under attack during the day, and as a consequence, many of the trips to the airport were at night, but the nightly trips could also be very dangerous, so for these trips, the vehicles of choice were APCs (Armored Personnel Carrier). An APC was well armed and provided security for the airport runs. Staff Sergeant Stefani was often the senior NCO for the airport trips, and he assigned machine gunners to cover both sides of the highway. His reminder to his gunners was always, "If it moves, shoot it."

Captain Gregory's company had cleaned up so many towns and villages in the ensuing months that everyone lost count of the number. The clearing became so routine that the drill had the men on the verge of boredom. The officers and NCOs had to constantly remind everyone to stay alert, be vigilant, and concentrate on the task at hand.

On one patrol, Nicky B's platoon was approaching a small town with Lola in the lead. She began her routine of searching for roadside bombs while the Marines were still under cover in a wooded area. On a hilltop above the town was a group of Saddam supporters armed with rifles. When Lola came into view, the riflemen assumed she was a stray, but when they noticed the precise pattern of her movements, they realized what she was doing.

In an attempt to scare her away from the bomb locations, a rifleman with a silencer fired bullets near her hoping she would run away. Unfortunately, one of the bullets hit a hidden bomb and it exploded. Lola had begun to retreat when the bullets struck the ground around her, but when the bomb exploded, fragments from the bomb wounded her rear legs. She tried to crawl back to the Marines on her forelegs, but her progress was very slow.

When Nicky heard the explosion and saw what happened to Lola, he began running toward her. His buddies kept yelling for him to come back to the safety of the woods, but he kept running toward Lola. The riflemen in the trees opened fire on him, but he kept running. When he reached Lola, he picked her up, and a moment later a bullet hit his flak jacket and knocked him down. He was groggy but was able to crawl to protection from the gunfire, for himself and Lola, behind a building.

Nicky's platoon ran out of the wooded area and opened fire with everything they had on the riflemen. Minutes later, the enemy firing stopped. A squad of Marines ran up to the top of the hill, but all they found were dead bodies.

The platoon detonated all of the roadside bombs, and the town was cleared in the usual manner.

Gunny Ascenzio found Nicky and Lola behind a building. Fortunately, Nicky had only some superficial wounds and would recover quickly, but Lola needed some expert treatment from a vet. Nicky carried Lola to a vehicle and held her there until the town was cleared.

Jimmy Geracollo drove Nicky and Lola to an Iraqi vet that treated Lola.

The vet found that some small fragments from the bomb explosion had damaged the ligaments, tendons, and cartilage of Lola's rear legs. He picked out pieces of metal and damaged cartilage and then sewed together the ligaments and tendons. He placed a large, soft collar around her neck so that she could not probe her bandaged wounds with her tongue and teeth. The vet's final instruction was to keep Lola lying down as much as possible and return in six weeks for a follow up examination.

Back at camp, the Marines fashioned a kind of crib for Lola to rest in. Every day, all day, a Marine would watch Lola, talk to her, and when possible, play with her.

15

Going Home

Six weeks after Lola was wounded, Nicky B took her back to the vet for a checkup. The doctor removed the bandages from her legs and took some x rays. After he completed his examination of her, he gave Nicky his evaluation. "Your dog is healing quickly because she is young, but she is not one hundred percent, and there may be some long-term impairment due to the loss of cartilage in her joints. She is allowed to walk, but if she tires, she will stop and sit down. Don't push her to get more exercise than she can handle. She knows better than you when enough is enough. Don't let her jump up and down from heights because that action may result in further injury to her leg joints. Keep her off her legs while she is resting. She can go out on missions with you, but keep a close eye on her and keep her out of danger. Do you have any questions?"

"I think you covered all the bases doctor. Thanks for your help. I hope I never need your services again."

Nicky paid the bill in American dollars, which were more valuable than the Iraqi currency.

The Marines spent the next few months engaged in a variety of assignments, some of which were shootouts with rebellious insurgents, and others which were theoretically less dangerous, but nevertheless, required vigilance and caution, like guarding large shopping markets and bazaars, along with helping at reconstruction sites and patrolling around oil pipelines.

Other than the shootouts, the most common dangerous assignments were at the markets, bazaars, and pipelines because of suicide bombers and planted explosive devices. In both cases, the purpose was to detonate the bombs in areas where they would cause the most damage and death. It was most important to prevent suicide bombers from getting in the middle of large crowds and the placement of bombs in the most vulnerable areas. For these reasons, the Marines patrolled the perimeter of the areas they were guarding. The purpose was to prevent a bomber from gaining access to his target location, and in case of an explosion, it would be on the perimeter where damage, injury, and loss of life would be kept to a minimum.

Lola played an integral part in the security process. She would casually move among those entering the protected zone, attempting to identify anyone carrying a bomb. When she identified a suspect, she would trail along behind that person. When the Marines recognized her signal and were alerted to the danger, they would move in to neutralize the situation.

The Marines had developed techniques to cope with a wide variety of scenarios. Some of the Marines were dressed in the local attire and circulated in the crowd. When a suicide bomber was spotted, a pair of Marines would move next to him, one on either side. If the bomber had his thumb on a plunger ready to detonate the explosive at the right moment, one of the Marines would slightly jostle the bomber to momentarily distract him while the other lifted the bomber's thumb off the explosive and broke it. The plunger would fall harmlessly, and the bomber would be escorted to a safe area.

When a person trying to plant a bomb was exposed, he would be detained and removed to a safe place. All bombers would be relieved of their explosives, and the explosives would be handled by a bomb disposal squad. The captured would be taken into custody by the appropriate judicial authorities and incarcerated.

If Lola identified a bomber entering a construction site, that person would be detained and treated like all other bombers. If the person resisted arrest, he would be severely disciplined and would have many reasons to rue his decision. If he attempted to escape, he would be shot dead.

In any potential bombing situation, there was always the possibility that the bomb could be detonated remotely. Fortunately for Lola and the Marines, that possibility was never realized.

16

No One Left Behind

During the spring, summer, and into the fall, Gregory's Marines and Lola completed all their missions. The company suffered several wounded, but no one was killed in the process. It was odd that no replacements for the wounded were sent to fill the vacant slots, and this anomaly led to rumors that the company would be disbanded and the men sent as replacements to other units, but by early October, word filtered through the chain of command that the company was being rotated back to the States before the end of November. The Marines cheered the news, but their enthusiasm was dampened by the possibility that the story might be more scuttlebutt.

As the days passed in October, the possibility of rotation became more and more likely. All except one of the Marines were flying high when they realized they might be going home soon. Nicky B was in a quandary. He wanted to go home, but he wanted to stay with Lola more, so he went to Captain Gregory and asked if he could be transferred to another Marine unit that was staying in Iraq. Gregory answered the query with, "That's not possible."

Nicky was not about to give up on Lola, so he asked, "Can I reenlist on the condition that I stay in Iraq until the end of my enlistment?"

Gregory did not answer the question, but he understood Nicky's concern, so he responded, "What makes you think that your new commanding officer will accept the package of you and Lola? He may say, 'I'm happy to have you in my unit, but you have to get rid of the dog.' You would have no choice but to obey the order, and you'd be worse off than you are now. Our orders say the entire company rotates; no exceptions."

"I have to do something. I can't just leave Lola behind. If I do, she'll be right back where she started from in this fucked up country, and everything she has done for this company will soon be forgotten by everyone except me."

Captain Gregory became concerned that Nicky might be contemplating going AWOL (Away without Official Leave) or deserting with Lola, so he tried to calm Nicky. "Don't do anything stupid. Give me a few days to look into this and see what I can do to help you out."

When Lola first became part of the company, Gregory wasn't crazy about the idea. He always worried that he would get his ass reamed by a superior for allowing a stray dog to participate in Marine missions, but after observing Lola's contributions to the missions and reducing the list of casualties, he went full circle and became an ardent supporter of her. He was determined to protect her from the bureaucratic bullshit that was a large part of any military organization.

The next day, Captain Frank Gregory USMC, dressed in full uniform, appeared at the Army post that made arrangements for the transportation of service dogs. Frank knew that service dogs were trained in the United States and then sent overseas, and he also knew that most of the dogs were not returned to the States, but he was confident that his argument would prevail.

At the front desk, an Army specialist was busy shuffling through paperwork, so Frank interrupted him, "Specialist, I'm here on orders from my superior Marine Corps Lieutenant General Victor Cannizzero. The General wants you to send his family dog back to the United States."

The soldier didn't hesitate to respond, "I'm sorry, sir, but I cannot help you. Dogs are only returned to the States under special orders signed by my superior."

"Who is your superior?"

"Colonel Janok."

"Soldier, if you don't help out with my assignment, I'll have to cover my ass, I'm not taking the fall if the dog isn't sent home, so this is what I'll have to do. I'll be forced to return here tomorrow with General Cannizzero and Colonel Janok and have them order you to comply with this request. Is that the way you want me to handle this?"

"It won't be necessary for those gentlemen to appear here tomorrow, sir."

The specialist gave Captain Gregory a form to fill out and a list of instructions for completing the form, and then he added, "Complete the form and have General Cannizzero sign it in the appropriate place. Bring back the completed form and the dog tomorrow, and I'll take care of everything else."

Captain Gregory called Nicky B into his office. Nicky was expecting the worst kind of news, but Gregory put him at ease and then spoke to him. "Lola is going back to the States with some other dogs. I have started filling out this form, but I need some information from you. What state do you want the dog sent to?"

"New York."

"Who will be responsible for picking up the dog?"

"My mother, Rosemarie Basasasvilli."

"Give me her address."

"115-07 Wentworth Boulevard, Albertson, New York."

"I put down that Rosemarie is the sister of the person signing this form."

"That's okay with me. Who is signing the form?"

"General Cannizzero."

"Who's he?"

"It's better that you don't know who he is. You can't get in trouble for what you don't know. I think that covers it. There's a note in the instructions that Lola will be kept in quarantine when she arrives in the States for thirty days at Fort Totten in Bayside, New York. It says here that the receiver, Rosemarie, can visit the dog while she is in quarantine. Is Albertson near Bayside?"

"Close enough. I'm sure my mother will visit Lola before she picks her up and takes her home."

"Good. Tomorrow I will take this form and Lola to the Army post. I'm sure there'll be no problems processing her. If there is nothing more, you're excused."

"Yes sir, I don't know how to thank you for saving Lola."

"You can thank me by continuing to do your job, Marine."

The next day Gregory passed the completed form to the specialist and asked, "Is the paper work in order."

The soldier looked to see if the form was signed and then stamped it "Approved." Captain Gregory gave Lola to the man and said, "Thank you for your help."

The soldier came back with, "It's a pleasure to be of service to the Marine Corps." He then added, "She'll be on her way today or tomorrow."

The captain had the last word when he commented, "If the Marine Corps can ever be of help to the Army, don't hesitate to ask."

17

Terra Firma

Lola's new mistress had been to visit her three times while she was in isolation at Fort Totten. The two were not able to come in contact with each other, but after the first visit, Lola recognized Rosemarie immediately on the subsequent visit and came as close to her as the confined space allowed. The bond between them had begun.

Pickup day for Lola after her quarantine ended was on Monday the week before Thanksgiving Day. Rosemarie carried Lola to her car as Lola tried to snuggle next to her rescuer, liberator, and protector. At home, Rosemarie let Lola roam around so she could get used to her new surroundings. For Lola, the explorations were of very short duration. Each episode of discovery lasted for about ten seconds, and then Lola would return to Rosemarie's side. The bonding process continued.

Rosemarie was prepared to care for Lola because she remembered her experiences with the original Lola on her father's dairy farm upstate, so she fed Lola, and the dog wolfed down her meal with relish. For the rest of the day, Rosemarie went about her chores while Lola trailed behind her.

Nicky B's company of Marines was reassigned to the Marine Corps base at Quantico, Virginia. The posting seemed odd to the Marines because they thought that they would be sent back to Camp Lejeune, but it was not to be.

Everyone in the company had accrued leave while in Iraq, and many of the men applied for leave so that they could celebrate Thanksgiving Day with their families.

Most of the requests for leave were granted, but regulations required that some men had to stay behind to handle company duties. Nicky was one of the lucky ones to get leave, and on the Monday before Thanksgiving Day, he arrived at home.

When Nicky walked into his home through the front door, Lola ran to him and jumped up on to his chest. While he was holding Lola, his mother came over to him, hugged and kissed him, and welcomed him home. After a short conversation between mother and son, Rosemarie returned to the kitchen where she was making lunch for her family. Nicky was still holding Lola and talking to her when he noticed that every few seconds Lola would turn her head toward Rosemarie to make sure she was still in the vicinity. After a few of Lola's head turns, Nicky realized that his dog was more interested in his mother's attention than his, and he thought to himself, "My mother stole my dog."

As the leave days flew by, Nicky gradually began to understand the strong bond that had developed between his mother and his dog. Each day Nicky took Lola for her routine walks so she could do her business and they could get reacquainted. Both man and dog enjoyed the experiences, but each time they returned home, the first thing that Lola did was make a beeline for Rosemarie and hang out with her.

In the beginning, Nicky was upset at the loss of Lola's affection and friendship because he had invested so much of his love in her. The Sunday after Thanksgiving Day, Nicky was packing his bags for the trip back to Quantico the next day. He was sad at the thought of leaving his family and Lola, but at the same time, he had come to the conclusion that Lola's staying with his parents and sister was the best possible situation for her. He also realized that Lola might not be welcome by the Marine Corps in the United States. There were too many rules and regulations that were not enforced in Iraq, and he knew his family would take better care of Lola than he could because he had to complete his enlistment, and no one knew where that would take him.

When he left for his return trip, he was content with the knowledge that things would work out for the best for everyone involved.

Part Seven

18

Reunion

When all of Captain Gregory's company was reassembled after the leaves were over, the guesswork ended. There was a reason why the men went from Iraq to Quantico as Gregory explained. "The Pentagon, in its wisdom, if you believe such a thing exists, has decided that we will be the lab rats in one of its studies."

Although the citizens of the country would not learn until later, the military was concerned with the effects of fighting a different kind of war on those who fought it. In Iraq, the use of suicide bombers, roadside bombs, and IEDs (Improvised Explosive Device) accounted for a great number of the wounded who suffered the loss of limbs and TBI (Traumatic Brain Injury).

After rotating back to the States, many of the combat veterans from Iraq suffered from PTSD (Post Traumatic Stress Disorder), drug addiction, alcoholism, and suicide, much like their comrades who fought in Vietnam.

Captain Gregory's company was selected to participate in a study of the effects of combat because they had been involved in a wide variety of adventures in Iraq. The Marines would travel to Bethesda Naval Hospital in Washington D.C. where they would have physical examinations, blood tests, interviews with psychologists and psychiatrists, and counseling sessions.

Each day a couple of squads would be bused to the hospital for a visit. After going through the drill, those that presented no issues would return to Quantico, while those in need of treatment would remain in the hospital until discharged.

On the third day of testing, Jimmy Geracollo found himself on a bus heading for the hospital. When the busload of Marines was discharged, the group was led to a large waiting room. The men sat in rows of folding chairs and waited for their names to be called. A nurse appeared and starting calling names and assigning testing stations. On the second roll call, Jimmy, who was sitting in the last row, heard his name called, so he moved forward to the nurse. The woman was reading from a clipboard with her head lowered, and when Jimmy appeared next to her, she said, "Geracollo, room 10."

Jimmy hesitated. The nurse's voice sounded familiar, but he could not recognize the downcast face. He was about to move on when it dawned on him, so he spoke to the nurse, "Is that you Nora?"

The nurse was so used to rattling off names that the name Geracollo did not register with her, but when Jimmy spoke to her, she immediately made the connection and looked up with a smile on her face and asked, "Is that you Jimmy? How are you?"

They looked at each other without saying a word until Nora broke the silence, "You look good, Jimmy, but you better move along now. We both have a job to do."

Before Jimmy moved toward room 10, he found his tongue, "You look good too Nora. I'll see you later."

When Jimmy finished the hospital routine, he returned to the waiting room, where he found Nora doing paperwork at the front desk. They chatted with each other, catching up on the last several months. The PA broke into their conversation notifying the Marines that it was time to get back on the bus. Jimmy mustered his courage and asked, "Nora, can I have your phone number. I'd like to see you again?"

Nora took a page from a script pad and wrote her name and phone number on it and added a note, "It was good to see you today. I'd like to see you again, and I hope you call. Until the next time."

"Thanks. I'll call real soon." On the ride back to Quantico, Jimmy kept reading Nora's note over and over again.

Jimmy planned to call Nora at the end of the week after he had secured a weekend pass. We all know what happens to the best laid plans of men. Jimmy's weekend pass was denied. He was afraid to call Nora with what he thought was a lame excuse like "No weekend pass." He assumed that she would assume that he didn't want to see her. The reader knows what happens when we assume.

The following week, Jimmy applied for a weekend pass, and it was granted, so he called Nora, who answered her phone on the second ring and heard, "I'd like to see you this weekend."

Nora was glad to hear from Jimmy, but she didn't want to seem too enthusiastic, so she responded, "Who is this?"

Jimmy was flustered because he thought Nora had other dates and that she had forgotten about him. After a short pause, he answered, "Jimmy Geracollo."

"Oh, it's you. I thought you had forgotten all about me."

Jimmy started to explain, "I couldn't get …."

Nora cut him off in midsentence, "You don't have to explain what happened. Things happen. I'd like to see you too this weekend, but if you don't show, forget about calling me again."

"I'll be there even if I have to go AWOL."

They made arrangements to meet at a local watering hole near the hospital. Nora arrived fifteen minutes before the appointed time and then went to the bar and ordered a drink. A half hour later, Jimmy had not yet arrived and Nora thought, "He stood me up, the bastard."

Nora was going to finish her drink and leave when Jimmy came flying through the door. He gasped as he tried to catch his breath and blurted out, "I'm glad you're still here; I got lost; I had to park five blocks away and I ran all the way over here; I'm sorry I'm late." He sat on a bar stool trying to catch his breath.

Nora was so glad to see Jimmy that she let her anger subside and disappear, so she responded to his outburst, "It's okay. Catch your breath, and when you're ready, we'll get a few drinks and enjoy the night."

Jimmy and Nora took their drinks from the bar and found a table in a quiet corner of the restaurant. They spent the next few hours exchanging recollections of their experiences since they last talked aboard the USS Falcony. While they chatted, they shared plates of finger food and ordered more drinks.

When it was time to call it a night, Jimmy asked Nora, "How did you get here? Do you want a ride home?"

"I live near the hospital, and after work I went home to shower and change my clothes. Then I walked here. It's nice of you to offer me a ride home. I accept."

Together they walked the five blocks back to Jimmy's parking spot, and he drove her back to her apartment building. Jimmy put his arm around Nora, and she moved closer to him. They began cuddling, kissing, and petting, but when the caressing became hot and heavy, Nora broke away from Jimmy and said, "Whoa, we need to take a break. This is getting out of hand. We're putting on an exhibition for my neighbors."

Jimmy was not in a mood to end the night on that note, so he asked, "Do you want to invite me up for a nightcap?"

"As appealing as that idea is to me, I can't do that."

"Why?"

"I live with a roommate who would not take kindly to my inviting a man into our apartment, if you catch my drift."

Jimmy's only comment was, "We'll have to do something about her."

Nora rearranged her hair and clothing and then said, "I'm going in now. It was fun. Let's do it again sometime."

"I'll call you."

"You'd better."

Jimmy watched Nora as she entered the apartment house lobby. She turned and waved to him and then headed for the elevator.

As Jimmy drove away from Nora, he muttered to himself, "Shit, I hate roommates."

19

Love Blooms

Jimmy's first date with Nora was on December 13 and the second one was a week later on the 20th. They met in the late morning and acted like tourists visiting some of the historic sites. In the middle of the afternoon, they stopped at a pub for a hamburger and a beer and then continued their tour, which lasted for the rest of the afternoon.

In early evening, they found a quiet café and decided to have dinner there. They ordered before dinner drinks as they read the menu. For dinner, they each ordered a salad, a red meat entrée, and a bottle of red wine that they shared.

When Jimmy drove Nora home, he parked his car in front of her apartment house. Instead of kissing her good night, hoping against the odds that he would get the answer he wanted to hear, he asked, "Can I walk you up to your apartment?"

Nora hoped he would ask for a nightcap. She was prepared to grant his request, but he had asked a different question, and she did not respond to it immediately. She had another surprise in store for him, which she kept to herself for the time being. Moments later, she answered his question by saying, "You're a real gentleman. Yes, you can walk me to my apartment. I would enjoy that."

At her apartment door, Nora fumbled for her keys on purpose. She wanted to delay her surprise for as long as possible. When she found her key, she dropped it on the floor. Jimmy bent down and picked up the key. When he tried to hand it to her, she said, "Why don't you open the door. My roommate is at her college reunion."

Jimmy put the key in the lock and turned the tumbler while asking, "Is this some kind of joke?"

"No, it's for real. My roommate is staying with friends for the weekend. Just open the door. I have to go to the ladies room."

Jimmy was more shocked than he had ever been in any combat situation, but he recovered quickly and opened the door. When they entered the living room, Nora asked, "What do you think of it?"

"It's much nicer than any place I've ever been in."

Nora showed Jimmy the bar and invited him to partake. "Make yourself a nightcap if you want one. I need to get to the bathroom."

Jimmy was not in the mood for a nightcap. He was in the mood for something more appealing to him. He couldn't believe his good fortune, and he was praying that his luck would hold up for a few more hours.

When Nora came back into the living room, she was scantily clad in a pair of shorts and a t-shirt. She was the most beautiful woman Jimmy had ever seen. He was seated on the couch, but stood up when she entered the room. Nora moved closer to him and they embraced. In seconds, their clothing began to fly about before landing on the floor. Naked, they fell on the couch together and did what lovers do. They spent the next few hours pleasuring each other.

Sometime around midnight, Nora said, "I think we should move into the bedroom. What do you think?"

"I'm a Marine. I don't think. I just follow orders. Lead the way."

In the bedroom, they continued their mattress gymnastics until just before dawn. They slept entwined with each other until a strong morning sun forced them awake. They clung to each other for a while, and then continued their lovemaking.

Around noon, Nora asked, "Do you want to have something to eat?"

"That's not a bad idea. What do you have in mind?"

"I think we should go out. The only things we have in the apartment for breakfast is coffee, tea, milk, and juice; no solid food."

They showered, dressed, and headed for a local bar that served brunch. The night's work had made both of them hungry, so they refueled on Bloody Marys, eggs, bacon, sausage, rolls, and buns. When they had satisfied their appetites, they returned to the apartment and sat on the couch together. They watched the news on TV and allowed the digestive process to work on the overload.

In mid-afternoon, feeling refreshed and energetic, they resumed their lovemaking. Hours after darkness fell, reality set in. It was time to part company. Jimmy had to be at roll call at 6:00 a.m. the next morning, and Nora had to be at work at the hospital by 7:00.

As Jimmy and Nora were saying their goodbyes, Nora thought, "Well, that was better than I had hoped for. I hope there is a lot more of that to come."

While Jimmy was driving back to Quantico, he thought, "That was great. I'd like to keep doing that forever."

The following Saturday was five days before Christmas, so Nora and Jimmy went Christmas shopping. They shopped from late morning until late afternoon with a break for lunch. Laden with presents, Jimmy asked Nora, "What are we going to do with all this stuff?"

"We can put them in my apartment. My roommate is at the Naval Academy for a conference."

"Why didn't you tell me that yesterday? We could have spent last night together."

"If we spent last night together, one thing would have led to another, and we wouldn't have done any Christmas shopping today."

They returned to the apartment, stored the presents, and enjoyed some afternoon delight. When their passions subsided, they showered together, dressed, and went out to dinner. After dinner, they went back to the apartment and resumed their love making, with a few bouts of sleep in between, until the next morning.

Around noon on Sunday, they went out for brunch and then returned to the apartment to satiate their passions. When darkness fell, Nora told Jimmy, "My roommate will be back soon. You'd better go."

Jimmy was exhausted and realized he needed a good night's sleep if he was going to be able to do his job on Monday, but he was reluctant to leave, so he responded, "Yes ma'am. Whatever you say."

Both Nora and Jimmy had been granted four days of leave. The leaves were from Christmas Eve to the following Sunday. Both planned to visit their families for the holidays.

Nora and her mother were in the kitchen making Christmas dinner when her mother asked Nora, "Are you still seeing that Navy officer you met aboard ship?"

"No."

"What happened?"

"We went out a few times when we both were assigned shore duty. There wasn't very much to that relationship. He wasn't the kind of guy I wanted in my life. His ego was too big for me to handle."

"Are you seeing anybody else now?"

"Yes, a Marine Corporal I met aboard the same ship." (Jimmy had been promoted just before he left Iraq).

"Isn't dating an enlisted man a violation of regulations?"

"Yes, but we keep our relationship between ourselves. Nobody else knows about us."

"Be careful, not only about you relationship, but also about your Marine. The Marines have a notorious reputation when it comes to women, and they're known to do some very crazy things, even when they are not on a battlefield. Keep a close eye on him and watch your step."

"Jimmy will always protect me, and he will never harm me. He's a keeper."

On the Monday night following their leaves, Jimmy called Nora, and when she answered, he spoke, "I have tickets for a New Year's Eve party. Can you get New Year's Day off?"

"Where's the party."

Jimmy gave her the name of the hotel. It was one of the nicer places in Washington, but not one of the elite.

"That sounds nice. I'm sure I'm off on New Year's Day."

Jimmy would be off on the 31st after his shift and had New Year's Day off. He was looking forward to a special night.

During the party, when they were dancing together, Nora said to her partner, "This is a very nice party. Thanks for inviting me. I don't want to put a damper on the evening, but I think you should know my roommate is back in town."

"Fear not woman, your hero has come to your rescue. I booked a room for us at this hotel. We don't have to go anywhere."

"My hero, you saved a damsel in distress." She kissed him on the cheek.

Shortly after the clock struck twelve, they went up to their room, which was much nicer than her apartment bedroom. Without fanfare or clothing, they engaged in activities that came naturally to lovers.

When checkout time arrived, they dressed in casual clothes and repacked their evening wear. Jimmy dropped Nora off at her apartment house after they said their goodbyes. They were both forlorn at parting, but they both agreed it had to be done. As Nora walked to the elevator, she prayed, "I hope nothing bad ever happens to us."

Jimmy, for his part, prayed to his guardian angel, "Take good care of her. I want to spend the rest of my life with her."

Part Eight

20

Making Plans

During the winter months, Nora and Jimmy met each other as often as commitments would allow. They went sightseeing, to museums and art galleries, to movies, and theatre matinees. For sustenance, they ate in bars, pubs, and restaurants. Not only did they spend their days together, but they spent every possible night together in bed.

When Nora's apartment was not available, they rented motel and hotel rooms. On many occasions, they had the use of apartments or homes of friends who would be away for the weekend. These were the kind of friends who didn't ask questions. It is a wise person that doesn't ask a question he doesn't want the answer to.

To avoid exposure, they kept moving their activities further away from Nora's workplace and apartment.

By spring, their relationship was at a very serious stage. They both wanted to be with each other every day, so they planned to take a cruise when they knew that they could get leave time.

When the cruise plans were finalized, Jimmy said to Nora, "This cruise was a great idea. I'll have a special surprise for you on the trip."

Nora's intuition told her what Jimmy already knew. He would ask her to marry him and present her with an engagement ring. For her part, Nora would play it cool and happily accept his offer by saying "Yes" to the proposal, while her love for him would be at the boiling point.

A few weeks before their cruise was to set sail, they were enjoying a quiet dinner in a small town outside of Washington when a young man walked up to their table and asked, "How are you doing Nora?" Nora looked up at the man and was horrified. She could not speak.

Months earlier, Nora knew that Jimmy was the love of her life, and he was madly in love with her, so in the spirit of full disclosure and clearing up the past, she asked, "Do you remember Ensign Settie from the trip to Spain?"

"Yes, I remember that dickhead asshole. What about him?"

"I just want to let you know that after that trip, I was assigned to Bethesda, and he was sent to the Pentagon. He kept in touch with me, and I had a few dates with him; nothing serious. I thought I would never see you again, so I took a shot with him, but he wasn't for me. His ego was bigger than the ship we were on. Finally, I broke it off with him. I thought you should know about him."

"If it's over it's over. I'm not going to waste my time thinking about that loser."

Nora realized that her worst nightmare had appeared before her in reality. When she was able to regain her composure, she responded to the question asked in a rather loud voice, "What are you doing here?"

When Jimmy heard the alarm in Nora's voice, he dropped his fork and looked up at the man who had shocked Nora and recognized Ensign Settie immediately, and he did not hesitate to speak to the man who had intruded. "Get the hell out of here sailor."

"That's not a very polite welcome Marine. I came to see the two of you, and now it's just the three of us." The man took a chair from a nearby table and sat down.

"How did you find us?" was Nora's concern.

"You can thank your roommate for that. I ran into her the other day, and she told me that you were having an affair with a man named James Geracollo."

"I never met the woman. She doesn't know anything about me."

"You two would make very lousy spies. She found motel, hotel, and restaurant credit card receipts in Nora's bedroom dresser. Some of the receipts were signed by Nora, and some by James Geracollo.

"I tracked the places you two frequented. You have eaten in this restaurant before, so here I am."

Jimmy was irate and on the verge of losing his self-control, but he was able to rein in his temper and calmly said, "We don't want anything to do with you. It's time for you to leave."

"Leave, I think not. You'll be leaving before I do."

"Pick yourself up and leave quietly, or I'll pick you up and throw you out; your choice."

"Let me explain something to you, tough guy. You're no longer in charge here. I am. Say good night to the lady and be on your way. It's all over between the two of you."

The argument between the two men was getting louder and creating a disturbance in the dining room, and the manager was moving to quell the outburst when Nora decided to take control of the situation, so she said to Jimmy, "Let me take care of this. Why don't you head home, and I'll call you tomorrow."

The last thing that Jimmy wanted to do was to leave Nora alone with this ego maniac. He had never retreated from a battle before, and he wasn't ready to start now. He wanted to kill this wimp sailor, who had dared to interfere in the life that he and Nora had built. He was about to take action when Nora pleaded with him, "Please Jimmy, I can handle this guy."

Jimmy did not want to argue with Nora and create a spectacle that would embarrass her, so he got up and left.

Nora blamed this confrontation on herself for being so stupid as to leave the signed credit card receipts in her bedroom for her roommate to find. She should have destroyed them, but she couldn't do anything about that now, so she said to the intruder, "My roommate had no right to go through my personal things."

"I kind of encouraged her to do it. I suspected you were up to something when you didn't answer or return my calls, and you know how lesbians are. They have to protect their turf."

The conversation between Dick and Nora continued quietly for a short time. The waiter cleared the dinner plates, and Dick ordered coffee for both of them.

After the waiter served the coffee and left the table, Nora asked, "What do you want from me?"

"This is the way it's going to be. You will break off your relationship with that jarhead tomorrow. You will be available to go out with me whenever I call you. Understand that you are my girl. If you don't do exactly as I say, I'll create problems for both of you."

"I don't think I can do that."

Nora called for the check and paid it. Dick never offered to pay the check. He wasn't about to pay for a dinner he didn't eat.

Nora took out her cell phone and was about to dial a number when Settie asked, "What are you doing?"

"I'm calling a taxi to take me home."

"Don't do that. I'll take you home."

Nora did not want to exacerbate the situation and further antagonize him, so she put her phone back in her pocketbook and said, "Okay, let's do it your way."

On the drive back toward Nora's apartment, Dick asked Nora, "Well, what's your decision? Are you going to dump that maggot Marine?"

"No, I'm not going to do it. I love Jimmy, and I want to marry him. It's all over between us."

As they were passing in front of Bethesda Hospital, Nora's work place, Settie suddenly made a hard right turn onto the hospital grounds and parked in the near empty hospital lot behind the building. Nora became confused and scared, and then asked, "What are we doing here?"

"I want to give you one last chance to change your mind about me. If you don't do things my way, I'll let the Navy and the Marine Corps know that you two are fraternizing. Both of you know it's against regulations for the enlisted to date officers. You will lose your commission and receive a less than honorable discharge from the Navy. I don't know what the Marine Corps will do with your beloved, and I don't care. They'll probably give him a medal for rising above his station. You're the one who will suffer the most in the end. Do it my way. It's the best decision for all of us."

"Not a chance. I love Jimmy, and I'm going to marry him. You and I are through." Nora pulled on the handle of her door and suddenly realized it was locked and that Dick was moving closer to her. She was now panicked and understood she was locked in the car with a deranged man. In an effort to escape her prison, she ordered, "Unlock this door! I'm getting out and walking home."

21

Until Death Do Us Part

Jimmy left the restaurant and sat in his car in a state of rage for many minutes. He wanted desperately to go back into the building, drag Settie out to the parking lot, and then pummel the impudence out of him until he begged for mercy. He knew that taking such action would have calamitous results for both himself and Nora, but he didn't care about the consequences. This man was about to ruin their lives. The thing that finally dissuaded him from doing what every fiber in his body wanted him to do was the knowledge that Nora would never forgive him for his recklessness, so he drove away from the restaurant still fuming.

Jimmy had no desire to return to the barracks at Quantico because his state of agitation would raise questions that he did not want to discuss or answer. He stopped at a bar just outside the gates of the base and parked his car in the lot. The bar had a very small crowd that night because it was Saturday night and most of the Marines were in other places on dates in anticipation of things to come in the early morning hours with members of the opposite sex.

Our hero headed for the corner of the bar and took the stool that was usually occupied by Claude Jayson and ordered a beer. Jimmy sipped on his beer all the while brooding over the events of the evening. His only consolation was that he had faith in Nora to pacify Settie and then send him on his way, out of their lives. He took comfort in the knowledge that Nora was smart, persuasive, committed, and had the wiles that all women possessed to pacify an out-of-control man.

A body seated itself on the stool next to Jimmy, and the body asked, "How are you doing, Jimmy? What are you doing here? I thought you would be out on the town with your lady friend tonight."

"What lady friend?"

"The Navy nurse from the hospital; everybody knows about her. How's that going?"

"What do you mean everybody knows about her. I never mentioned a girlfriend to anyone?"

"It was very easy to figure out. You've been walking around like a love sick puppy for months."

"Was it that obvious?"

"More than you'll ever know. Where is she tonight, working, or did you two have a lovers' spat?"

They ordered several more rounds of beer while Jimmy told Gunny Ascenzio about his love story with Nora and the events of that night. When he was finished, Jimmy asked his mentor, "What do you think I should do now?"

Vince did not answer immediately. He wanted more information, so he asked a few questions for clarification. "Is this the same nurse that bandaged your hand on the trip to Spain? Is he the same Navy officer who caused you so much trouble on the same ship?"

"Yes to both questions."

"How did they both end up in Washington?"

"After the Spain trip, she was sent to Bethesda, and he was reassigned to the Pentagon."

"You had good luck with the girl and bad luck with the guy. I told you when all this first started that you were playing with fire, and now both you and Nora are in the frying pan. Both of you will probably get thrown out of the military. What will you do then?"

"We'll worry about that when the time comes. I need to know what I should do now."

"Get ready for civilian life. Seriously, don't do anything foolish. Wait and see if Nora can settle this situation quietly, no pun intended, and get that asshole off your back. Be careful and wait for her to call you. Her roommate may be listening to her phone conversations and reporting back to Settie." The two Marines walked back to their barracks.

Jimmy wasted away Sunday morning waiting for Nora's call, but the suspense was killing him when he hadn't heard from her by mid-afternoon, so he called her. She did not answer his call, and the phone did not direct him to leave a message on voice mail. He was beside himself and decided to drive to her apartment, but when he got to his car in the bar's parking lot, he changed his mind. Nothing would be gained if Nora wasn't in her apartment, so he drove his car back onto the base and waited.

After the patients were served breakfast at Bethesda and the staff had cleaned up after them on Sunday morning, a cafeteria worker was taking the garbage out to the dumpster behind the hospital. When he lifted the lid on the container and looked inside, he dropped his load of debris on the ground, gasped, stepped back, took out his cell phone, and dialed 911.

An operator answered and said, "Metropolitan Police Department. What is your emergency?"

"I just found a body in the garbage can."

"Who are you?"

"Tyrone, the cook."

"What is your location?"

"Location? I live at …."

"No, no! Where are you now?"

"Behind the hospital I work at."

"What is the name of the hospital you work at?"

"Bethesda, the Navy hospital here in Washington."

"Thank you, Tyrone. Don't hang up. I'll be back with you in a minute."

Tyrone stayed on the silent phone line while the operator dispatched a police car to the hospital. Then she came back on the line and said, "Thanks for hanging on, Tyrone. Don't touch or disturb anything at the scene and don't let anybody else near the body except the police who will be with you shortly."

"Police? Did I do something wrong?"

"No Tyrone, you didn't do anything wrong. The police have to secure the crime scene and investigate what happened to the body in the garbage can."

"Oh, is that how it works? I thought you would just send an ambulance to pick up the body."

"Is the body dead or alive?"

"Don't think it's alive. I've seen dead bodies before, and this one looks pretty dead to me. Like when my granny died."

"If the person is dead, I don't think the police will need an ambulance to move the body."

"I guess they'll bring a hearse for her. That would make more sense since the body is already dead."

"What is your family name, Tyrone?"

"My father's name was …."

"Not that. What is your last name?"

"It's Biggers. The police must be coming because I can hear sirens. I better hang up now. When they get here, the police will most likely want to talk to me."

"Thank you for your cooperation, Mister Biggers. Have a nice day."

"You're welcome. I always try to help the police. I'm a respected citizen."

The police car pulled up next to the dumpster, and Officer Pamela Fullerton stepped out. She walked over to the man standing by the dumpster and said, "You must be Tyrone Biggers. Is that right?" Tyrone nodded and Fullerton ordered, "Show me what you got."

Tyrone walked Pamela over to the dumpster and pointed inside. Pamela stood on her tiptoes, looked inside, and then stepped away saying, "Yep, looks dead to me."

She walked Tyrone away from the scene and told him to sit in the back of the police car. Tyrone thought the police officer was blaming the dead body on him, so he protested, "I'm no killer. Why you arresting me?"

"I'm not arresting you, Tyrone. I just want you out of the way while the police investigate what happened here. The detectives will let you go back to work after they have talked to you."

After Pamela got Tyrone settled in the back of the police car, she took out her cell phone and called the desk sergeant on duty.

When he answered, Pamela said, "You better send the detectives. It looks like we have a murder on our hands. I'll tape off the area."

Detectives Tommy Garlin and Jack Pelman of the MPD arrived at the scene and parked next to the police car. Officer Fullerton went over to greet them, and introductions were made. Detective Garlin opened his investigation by saying, "Show us the crime scene."

Fullerton led the detectives to the dumpster, pointed inside it, and said, "She's in there."

The detectives looked inside, saw the body of a young, naked woman, and stepped back. Pelman said to his partner, "I'll call the crime scene investigators and the medical examiner."

Garlin responded, "Good idea. The lady didn't die of natural causes or commit suicide, that's for sure."

The crime scene investigators searched the area around the dumpster and took samples of their findings, but they did not disturb the dumpster or its contents. That would have to wait until the body was removed from the container.

When the coroner, Doctor Jenny Capice, arrived, she was led to the body and did a visual inspection of the scene before stepping away while commenting, "I can't tell much from here. You need to get the body out of there so I can examine her."

Garlin called over two CSIs who carefully lifted the body out of the dumpster, while trying not to disturb the other contents. They placed the body on a tarp away from the taped area, and the doctor began her examination. The CSIs could now begin their inspection inside the dumpster.

The detectives and the policewoman moved next to their cars where Tommy asked Pamela, "Who's that in the back of your car?"

"Tyrone Biggers. He found the body."

Garlin said, "I'll talk to Biggers. Jack, you go find out what you can from the doctor." Pelman did as he was ordered. "Fullerton, send Biggers over to me and then you can return to your command. I'll contact you if I need to speak to you again."

"Mister Biggers, what can you tell me about this situation?" Tyrone went through his whole story from beginning to end. The detectives took notes while Tyrone talked. When Tyrone finished his tale, Garlin handed him a card with his ID and phone number on it and said, "If you can think of anything else that might help us solve this crime, call me day or night. If I need to speak to you again, I'll contact you. Thank you for your help, Tyrone. You can go back to work now." Tyrone hastened away. He was glad to escape the area.

Garlin went over to where his partner and the doctor were speaking and asked, "What can you tell us doctor?"

"There is bruising around the neck area. The hyoid bone is fractured, and she has signs of retinal petechiae. That's the red and purplish spots in her eyes. They are all indications of strangulation. Your partner was just asking me what that thing is stuck in her neck. Looking at the handle, I would guess it's a tool of some kind, like a putty knife. It tore up the tissue around the wound, but it was probably done after she died. There was very little bleeding from the blood vessels in her neck because her heart had already stopped pumping before that was done. I'll know more when I do an autopsy. Call me later."

Tommy asked Jack, "Did you find any ID?"

"No."

Garlin walked over to the investigators and rephrased his question, "Did you guys find any ID for the woman?"

The chief investigator answered, "No wallet, pocketbook, or purse found in the dumpster or the area around it. The doc will take fingerprints and send us blood samples for DNA testing. She'll also send over that thing stuck in her neck. If she's in the system, we'll know soon who she is."

"Thanks. Let me know what you find the moment you find it."

"You got it. Talk to you later."

The doctor would arrange for the transportation of the body to the morgue where she would do her autopsy and investigators would clear the scene when they were finished. There was nothing left for the detectives to do at the crime scene, so they returned to their office to start writing up their reports.

Jimmy was frantic all day Sunday, but he decided to heed Vince's advice and not try to contact Nora again after his earlier attempt. After lights out, he tried to sleep, but with little success. He tossed, turned, and worried all night. At breakfast, he spoke to Gunny Ascenzio, "I never heard from Nora yesterday. I'm going out of my mind. I have to do something to find her."

"Sit tight. I have a meeting with Captain Gregory in an hour. I don't know what the meeting is all about, but after that, I'll find you, and together we'll try to find her. Don't panic. You're a Marine. Keep it under control. I'm sure there is a simple explanation for what happened to her."

When Ascenzio reported to Gregory, the officer said, "Take a seat Gunny. I have something very important to discuss with you. Do you know a Navy nurse named Nora Pettite?"

"Wasn't she the nurse who bandaged up Geracollo when he hurt himself on the Falcony?"

"It could be. This is what I know at the moment. I got a call early this morning from an Agent Worthy at NCIS (Naval Criminal Investigative Service) that a Lieutenant JG Pettite was found murdered behind Bethesda hospital. She probably was murdered on Saturday night. The MPD investigated the crime, and the coroner ID'd the victim. MPD called NCIS because the victim was Navy, so NCIS took over the case."

"I feel terrible about the woman, but what has that got to do with us?"

"There's more to the story. There was a tool described as a putty knife embedded in the woman's neck. The doctor examined the object and found traces of new and old blood stains on it. The doctor sent the object to CSI for testing. CSI found the newer blood belonged to the dead woman, but the older blood belonged to our Corporal Geracollo. I think Geracollo is in big trouble. Agent Worthy is coming over here to talk to the corporal. Keep your eye on him and make him available for Agent Worthy. Don't let him do anything stupid like going AWOL. If he tries to escape, stop him anyway you can. Arm yourself."

"Yes sir." Vince left Gregory's office, went to the armory, holstered a .45, and then went to find Jimmy. When he found the corporal, Jimmy asked, "What did the boss want to see you about. It must be serious since you're carrying a weapon?"

"He wanted to bring me up to date on a few things. Let's go to my office where we can talk."

When the men were seated in the office, Vince opened the conversation, "I've got some bad news for you Jimmy."

"What's the bad news? Are we going back to Iraq?"

"No, it's worse than that."

"What could be worse than that? C'mon, what could be worse than that?"

"The MPD found Nora's body yesterday. She was murdered."

Jimmy's face went ashen as he started to go into shock. All he could do was utter, "What happened?"

Vince recounted his meeting with Captain Gregory as Jimmy lapsed into despair, and his emotions became unhinged. He stood up and roared, "I have to get out of here and find the bastard who did this." Jimmy turned and moved toward the office door.

Vince was expecting Jimmy to do something like that, so he sprang out of his chair, cut Jimmy off before he could reach the door, bear hugged him, and said, "You're not going anywhere. An agent from NCIS is coming over to talk to you."

"Gunny, you gotta let me go. I can't stay here. I can't just sit here and wait. I have to do something."

Vince was still holding Jimmy tightly as he said, "Don't try to run away. If you do, I'll chase you down and knock you out, and if I can't catch you, I'll shoot you in the back." Vince patted his sidearm and then tightened his grip on his prisoner.

When Jimmy first heard the news about Nora, he was on the verge of tears, but when the enormity of those words were finally absorbed by his brain, the tears began to flow in earnest and the flood gates burst open. Jimmy punched Vince on his shoulders and the sides of his head, blows that Vince ignored because there was no power behind them in those close quarters and Vince had suffered no physical pain, only emotional pain and sympathy for his friend.

As Jimmy continued the pounding on his mentor, he began a tirade. "I hate God! Why did he let this happen? He should have taken me instead of her! She was a much better person than me! Why does he always take the good ones?"

"This is all Nora's fault. She brought this all on herself. She should have come home with me and none of this would ever have happened. No, she wanted to do it her way, and look what it got her. She should have let me take care of that prick and she'd still be alive. Now she's gone, and I'm all alone.

"I told my guardian angel to protect her, and what did he do. He fell asleep on guard duty. He's not a Marine guardian angel. He failed in his mission. I don't want anything to do with him anymore. He can go to hell for all I care and work for the devil.

"But I'm the worst of them all. I'm a miserable failure. If I couldn't save her, who can I save? Not my buddies when the shit hits the fan. No one can depend on me anymore. It's time for me to go find Nora and be with her in the next world."

Jimmy was emotionally and physically exhausted as he slid out of Vince's grip and fell on the floor semiconscious with his eyes wide open, staring into nothingness.

Vince left Jimmy on the floor as he curled up into a fetal position. Vince went back and sat in his chair with his head in his hands, watching his friend suffer unimaginable and unbearable pain.

Several minutes later, everything about Jimmy seemed to stop. Vince thought that Jimmy had given up the fight and died. He went over and tried to rouse the Marine. "Get up, get up!"

Jimmy came to life, as if roused from a dream, asking, "What's going on Gunny?"

"Jimmy, why don't you get up off the floor and sit in your chair?" With vacant eyes and without saying a word, Jimmy did as he was directed. The two men just looked at each other for several minutes.

A knock on the door broke the silence, and Vince ordered, "Enter."

Two men entered the room, and the first man identified himself. "I'm NCIS Agent Lou Worthy," and added, "this is my partner, Steve Bascanelli. We're here to see James Geracollo. Is he here?"

Vince pointed to Jimmy and answered, "That's him."

Agent Worthy stepped in front of Jimmy and asked, "Do you know a Nora Pettite?"

"Yes."

"How do you know her?"

"She's my girlfriend."

"When was the last time you saw her?"

"Saturday night."

"Can you tell us about the events of Saturday night?"

Jimmy, sometimes incoherently, related the story about what happened in the restaurant on Saturday night. He finished his story with, "I left."

"Your blood was found on the victim. You are a suspect in her murder. I'm placing you under arrest. You are going with us. Stand up."

Agent Bascanelli went to put cuffs on Jimmy, but Vince held up his hand saying, "That won't be necessary. I'm responsible for him, and since we're not leaving the base, we'll both go with you."

The agents escorted the two Marines to the brig where Jimmy was confined.

Vince found Master Sergeant Mercados, the NCO in charge of the jail, and started a conversation with him. "If it's alright with you, I want to send some of my men in here to assist your guards. I'll have one man on duty around the clock to keep an eye on Geracollo. I'm worried about him. He's in a bad place, and I don't want him to hurt himself or somebody else, or something worse."

"That's okay with me, but remind your men that my men are in charge here. I don't want any confrontations."

"You're in charge. We'll do it your way. My men won't cause any problems for you or your men."

Gunny Ascenzio turned in his weapon and returned to his office. He shuffled paperwork around, not accomplishing a damn thing because he was having a really lousy day.

Part Nine

22

Military Justice

The office of the Navy Judge Advocate General handled the legal matters for the Navy, Marine Corps, and Coast Guard, so NCIS Agent Worthy notified JAG that Marine Corporal James Geracollo was under arrest as a suspect in the murder of Navy Lieutenant JG Nora Pettite.

The case landed on the desk of Commander Theresa Scafidi. As she read the MPD and NCIS reports, she remembered Nurse Pettite from her time aboard the Falcony. The name Geracollo escaped her at the moment, but the word Marine rang a bell and she recalled the events aboard ship involving Pettite, Geracollo, and an Ensign Settie. The reports she read seemed to indicate that the two men, Geracollo and Settie, had both been in the company of the victim the night she died. She remembered Settie as an arrogant young man with a chip on his shoulder when it came to Marines. Settie had aggravated and harassed her with his complaints and recalled that the accusation against Geracollo came to nothing. She was happy to be rid of the pest and that his case had collapsed.

Knowing the history of the two men involved, Scafidi knew that she had to move forward carefully with this case if it led to a general court-martial. The last thing she wanted was for inter service rivalry to erupt in a courtroom.

Her legal training led her to her files and the notes of the episode aboard the Falcony. The reading of her notes prompted her to search the military database of Marine Corps officers. When she found what she was looking for, she dialed the number of Captain Frank Gregory, and when a man answered, she asked, "Is this the office of Marine Captain Gregory?"

"Yes it is ma'am. This is Captain Gregory speaking. What can I do for you?"

"I'm Commander Scafidi, Navy JAG. We met aboard the USS Falcony last year on a voyage to Spain. We worked on a case together involving one of your Marines and a Navy officer. Do you remember the incident?"

"Yes I do. It was much ado about nothing if I remember correctly. What can I do for you today?"

"I think I need your help on a case that was just handed to me. It involves your Marine Geracollo. I assume you know he is in custody and faces a disciplinary hearing."

"I'm aware of Geracollo's situation."

"Can we discuss his case?"

"You probably know more about the case than I do, but I know someone who is familiar with the case and can help you more than I can. Do you remember Gunnery Sergeant Vince Ascenzio?"

"Yes I do."

"Give me your phone number and I'll have him contact you."

Gregory called Ascenzio as soon as he got off the line with Scafidi and ordered, "Gunny, write this number down. It's the number for Commander Theresa Scafidi, a Navy JAG officer that we met on the Spain trip. Call her. I think she can help Geracollo with the mess he's in, and God knows he can use all the help he can get."

Gunny Ascenzio did as commanded and dialed the number he was given. When a woman answered his call, he addressed her, "This is Gunnery Sergeant Ascenzio. Is this Commander Scafidi?"

"Yes it is. Thank you for calling back so quickly, Gunnery Sergeant. Captain Gregory thinks you can help me with the Geracollo case. Can we meet?"

"I'm a bit confused. Are you the Lieutenant Commander Scafidi I met on the Falcony or a different Commander Scafidi?"

"I'm the same person. I was promoted last December, an early Christmas present."

"Congratulations Commander. I think it's a good idea for us to meet. What do you suggest?"

"Can you come to my office in DC?"

"I don't think that would be a good idea."

"Why not?"

"Some of your co-workers or bosses might think it unusual for you to be having a friendly conversation with an enlisted man when you're in charge of a Navy versus Marine Corps case. Remember we would both be in uniform."

"I see your point. It might raise some uncomfortable questions. Have you got a better idea?"

"I think we should meet in a public place in civilian clothes far away from Quantico and Washington. How about a restaurant? We will look like just two people having a business lunch."

"I like that idea. Let's do it."

They discussed the possibilities for a meeting place and decided on a restaurant that they both knew midway between their locations. When the decision was made on day and time, Scafidi ended the conversation with, "Well, that's settled. I'm looking forward to seeing you again."

Ascenzio and Scafidi met for lunch as agreed to. Vince arrived first and seated himself at a table in a remote corner of the restaurant because he knew their conversation would be confidential, and he didn't want any prying ears to be part of the conversation.

A few minutes after Vince had seated himself, Theresa arrived. He stood and waved her over to the table. When Theresa had seated herself, he welcomed her with, "I'm glad you could make it."

"I hit a little traffic, but I made it on time. How are you?"

"I'm fine. How are you doing?"

She answered with, "I'm as well as could be expected under the circumstances."

The waitress came over to the table and took their order. Theresa ordered a house special everything salad and a glass of white wine. He ordered a medium rare hamburger platter with a side order of fried onion rings and a pint of domestic beer.

When the waitress left with the order, Theresa started the conversation, "What can you tell me about Geracollo and his relationship with Pettite?"

Vince told her everything he knew about them from the beginning on the Falcony to the time Jimmy was arrested and incarcerated.

When the waitress served their food, they took several minutes to eat in silence. When Theresa was half way through her salad, she put her fork down and said to Vince, "This is a very sticky situation. I have to appear impartial, so there is very little I can do to control what happens next. My first step will be to appoint an officer to conduct an Article 32 hearing. With the evidence available, I'm almost positive a general court-martial will be recommended by the investigating officer."

"I know Jimmy didn't do it. I'm sure he'll be vindicated in the end. Don't do anything that will jeopardize your position at JAG. We don't want you rowing in the same boat with Jimmy."

"Relax, this isn't my first rodeo."

Vince wolfed down the rest of his meal in seconds while Theresa picked at the rest of her salad. After a few more forkfuls, Theresa dropped her fork into the salad bowl and said, "I can't eat any more. I better get back to work. Thanks for meeting me. I enjoyed getting out of the office."

Ever the gentleman, Vince waved the waitress over and said to her, "Check please."

When the waitress handed Vince the bill, he reached into his pocket, removed his wallet, and produced a credit card, but before he could give it to the waitress, Theresa interfered with the transaction by saying, "I'll take care of that. I can put it on my expense account."

Vince knew better than to disobey an officer, so he handed the bill to Theresa saying, "If you insist."

While she was tending to payment of their lunch, Vince returned the credit card to his wallet and replaced it in his pocket.

Vince walked Theresa to her car, opened the door for her, and when she was seated, he ended their meeting with, "It was good to see you again. Keep in touch." She drove back to Washington and he returned to Quantico.

* * * * *

The United States Code of Military Justice requires an Article 32 hearing, a hearing much like a preliminary hearing in civilian law, before a defendant can be referred to a general court-martial.

Commander Scafidi's responsibility was to assign a commissioned officer to conduct the Article 32 investigation. This investigating officer cannot be the accuser, Judge Advocate prosecutor, or an officer in the accused chain of command.

If Scafidi assigned an investigator from either the Navy or the Marine Corps, she would be accused of having a prejudice in favor of the selected service, so to avoid that conflict, she reached out to the other service in the Navy JAG command, the Coast Guard, and selected Senior Lieutenant Pat Matthews.

This wasn't the first time Matthews was a compromise candidate. Both the Navy and the Marine Corps had reached out to her before to avoid the appearance of bias. Her track record of success was not perfect, but her triumphs were far greater than her slumps. Oftentimes her investigations led from almost certain general court-martials to lesser outcomes where the defendant faced a summary court martial, special court martial, non-judicial punishment, or administrative separation.

Lieutenant Matthews knew how to conduct an investigation, and so she went about her job in an orderly fashion; practice makes perfect. She asked for, and received, copies of the MPD and NCIS reports from Commander Scafidi, read the reports, and then scheduled a hearing that was attended by Pat, the accused, and defense counsel and witnesses. All testimony was given under oath, and Geracollo was allowed to make an unsworn statement. All evidence gathered would be turned over to the prosecutor.

After the hearing, Matthews submitted her report to JAG with her recommendation.

When Commander Scafidi received a copy of the report, she skipped through the details of the report looking for Matthew's recommendation. What she found was what she expected to find. Matthews had recommended a general court-martial. Almost all of the evidence pointed to Jimmy as the killer.

Scafidi now had to move ahead with the assignment of the personnel needed to conduct the trial.

23

Defense Strategy

Commander Scafidi had two problems concerning the Article 32. The first she solved by assigning Pat Matthews as investigator, but the second was more complex. She needed to find counsel for Jimmy Geracollo. She looked at the list of JAG officers available and found that all of the senior and most experienced lawyers were not available to assume the duties of defense counsel at a general court-martial. They already had a full caseload. That left the young and inexperienced counselors. She looked over the list and decided that none of them could provide the kind of legal direction Jimmy needed.

She had decided to go to her last option to find an investigator, so for a defense counsel, she decided to go outside the box again and selected a civilian lawyer. Her choice was Carol Ann Garnett. The two women had gone to law school together and were still friends that kept in touch with each other.

Carol Ann was born in Canada. Her father was a Canadian Royal Marine when she was born. After his military service, he became a member of the RCMP (Royal Canadian Mounted Police), and after five years of policing, he moved his family to Boston, Massachusetts, where he took a job as a Boston policeman, and raised his family there.

Carol Ann was an honor student in elementary school and high school. After high school, she attended Boston College as a political science major. Not finished with higher education, she was admitted to Harvard Law School

Theresa and Carol Ann were both editors of the Law Review at Harvard. After graduation, Theresa was off to the military, and

Carol Ann was hired at a prestigious Boston law firm specializing in criminal defense.

At first Carol Ann handled a lot of misdemeanor and pro bono cases, and she spent a lot of time in night court as a result of her caseload. She watched and learned from the senior, experienced lawyers in the firm and quickly established herself as a very capable and successful litigator. During her second year, the firm assigned her high profile cases that she most often concluded in the defendant's favor.

While Carol Ann was learning her way around a civilian courtroom and learning the tricks of the legal trade, Theresa was learning how to find her way through summary, special, and general court-martials while avoiding the minefield of military justice idiosyncrasies.

Lieutenant Commander Scafidi was involved in a special court-martial of a young sailor that she had been assigned to as the military judge. Appraising the case, she was of the opinion that the sailor was going to be railroaded as an example to his enlisted shipmates.

As the appointed judge, Theresa had read the Article 32 report and saw that the sailor was defended by an assigned, inexperienced Navy lieutenant who would be out of his depth at court-martial trial, and that the sailor's case would be torpedoed and sunk, so she reached out to her law school classmate, Carol Ann Garnett.

"Carol Ann, this is Theresa Scafidi. I need your help with a case I'm involved in. I think the defendant is going to get the royal shaft at the hands of incompetent counsel."

"What's the case all about?"

Theresa went on to explain the situation and then asked, "Will you defend the sailor?"

Carol Ann's answer was, "Let me think about it. I'll call you tomorrow with an answer."

Carol Ann thought about Theresa's offer for a long time as she recalled the stories she had heard from her Royal Marine father about how enlisted people were always getting screwed by a panel of biased officers. She was always looking for new adventures, and she saw this as an opportunity to work in military law, which would expand her legal expertise, and at the same time satisfy her sense of daring.

The next day, she called Theresa and simply said, "I'll do it. What happens next?"

Lieutenant Commander Scafidi went to her supervisor and reported that Carol Ann Garnett would be counsel for the accused sailor. The current counsel for the sailor was relieved to learn that he was being replaced, and he understood why. He was in way over his head. On the flip side of the coin, his ego had difficulty in accepting the fact that he was being replaced by a civilian, and a woman at that, but he kept that feeling to himself.

Carol Ann enjoyed her first experience in a military courtroom, and she was very successful. The sailor only suffered the discipline of a Captain's Mast under Article 15, which ended in a reprimand

Now she was defending Jimmy and hoping to save him from a fate that could be death.

24

Meeting of the Minds

Carol Ann and Jimmy met at the Quantico brig in a private room set aside for lawyers and their clients. Carol Ann opened the meeting with, "We expected investigator Matthews to recommend a general court-martial, so now we have to deal with that reality and prepare for a trial that could end very badly for you. I'll do everything I can to defend you and get you acquitted of the murder charge, but I'm telling you at the beginning that it won't be easy. The evidence is stacked up against you."

From Jimmy, "How do you plan to start?"

"The prosecution will present its case first. I have a list of his witnesses, so we'll find out what they have to say and find out what direction he's going in. I'll cross examine any testimony that reflects negatively upon you in an effort to derail the prosecutor's strategy and make the jury panel have doubts about your guilt on the murder charge. I don't think you'll be completely exonerated on all the minor charges in the indictment. In my experience, a panel of jurors usually believes that if someone ends up at trial with a list of charges against him, he must be guilt of at least one or more of them."

"I guess my case is hopeless. I'll either end up before a firing squad or spend the rest of my life in prison. If I have a choice, I'll take the firing squad. That's what most fighting men would opt for."

"Never give up. There is always hope for success. I see some ways of building a case in your favor. Remember, you're a Marine, and a Marine never surrenders. Keep the faith."

"What ways?"

"The prosecution's case is entirely circumstantial. There are no witnesses to the murder. The only thing that connects you to the murder is the tool with your blood on it."

"The tool is a paint scrapper. That was the tool I was using to scrape paint on the ship when I injured myself."

"The paint scrapper with your blood on it could help us in an odd way. No sane murderer would leave behind a piece of evidence at a crime scene that could be traced back to the guilty party."

"It could also work against me. I'm a Marine, and the panel might believe, like many people do, that all Marines are somewhat crazy in one way or another."

"Let's hope that the panel doesn't subscribe to that opinion. If they do, they're not giving you a fair hearing, and everything will be lost."

"You keep using the word hope. If I was going to lead a life based on hope, I should have joined the priesthood instead of the Marine Corps."

"It's just an expression. I don't base my defense strategy on hope. I base it on the law and my experiences that have taught me how to win in a courtroom, but I never abandon hope or prayer."

"I hope you believe that I didn't kill Nora. I never would have. I loved her too much."

"I know that, and I'm going to prove it during the trial."

"What's the worst thing I have going against me at trial? Is it the paint scrapper?"

"No, it's Ensign Settie."

"Why him?"

"It depends on how the prosecutor prepares him for his testimony on the stand. The prosecutor will control his story in such a way that his testimony will try to convince the panel that you're the only one with a reason to kill Nora, probably because you were jealous of her relationship with Settie, and if you couldn't have her, nobody else could either."

"I know he killed Nora for the reason you just suggested about me. Is there any way you could shift the blame to him for the murder?"

"I very much doubt it unless he makes a very stupid mistake in what he says under oath."

"What kind of stupid mistake?"

"I don't know at this point, but if he makes a mistake during the trial, I'll know it when he does and I'll pounce on him at that moment."

"What's the best thing I have going for me?"

"Gunnery Sergeant Ascenzio's testimony."

"Why don't you put him on the stand early in the trial so he can give me an alibi for the time when Nora was murdered?"

"The only way that will happen is if the prosecution calls him as a witness for their side. I'd like to save him for the defense, hoping he can make a lasting impression on the panel of your innocence."

"He's my only hope. Shouldn't we plant the seed of my innocence early in the trial so everybody knows our side of the story?"

"Do you realize that you just used the word hope for the second time?"

"I didn't realize it when I said it, but I do now. I think you brainwashed me with your attitude, and let us hope that things work out our way."

"There you go again with that word hope. I see you haven't given up on your case yet."

"Get off my back counselor and give me a break. You know that I didn't graduate from high school, and I'm not good with words. I never mastered that skill like you and some other people I know. My thoughts and words are not always on the same page. Take me as I am, or don't take me at all. If you want to quit on me, I'll understand."

"I'm not a Marine, but I'm not a quitter either. Let's get back to your case. Early or late, it all depends on whether or not the people who will decide your fate believe Ascenzio's testimony."

"Why wouldn't they believe him?"

"Because you both belong to the same club."

Jimmy and Carol Ann spent some time going over some minor legal points and then ended their meeting. Jimmy went back to his cell, and Carol Ann back to her office. They both needed time to think, plan, and organize a game plan for the championship match.

25

General Court-Martial

Commander Scafidi had to be very careful in her assignments of the court-martial personnel. She needed to assign an officer judge, a prosecutor, and a seven-person jury panel, and she had to do it without it appearing that she favored either the prosecution or the defense.

For the prosecution, she assigned a Navy Lieutenant Commander Mike Frisolli, who had limited, but successful, experience.

The judge's position was filled by Marine Lieutenant Colonel Christina Hennessey. This appointment was made to prevent any collusion between the judge and the prosecutor.

To counter any objections to Hennessey's appointment, Scafidi appointed a seven-man jury panel. By regulation, the panel was required to have at least five members, but by appointing the seven, she hoped that it would appear that the Navy had an advantage. The panel consisted of three members of the Navy: a commander, a lieutenant commander, and a lieutenant. The Marine Corps was represented by a major and a captain. The final two slots were filled by two Coast Guard commanders whose service records indicated that they were never involved in a dispute between the Navy and the Marine Corps. Commander Scafidi conjectured that the guardsmen would be the most impartial jurors and could possibly shift the outcome of the trial in favor of the defense. Neither the prosecution nor the defense objected to the composition of the court. Everything was in place for the start of the court-martial.

Judge Hennessey had set a date and a time for the start of the trial, and on that date, both sides were in place when the judge appeared and was seated. The judge mentioned a few preliminary instructions to the trial's participants and then said, "Let's get started. Commander Frisolli, you're up."

Frisolli had his assistant pass out copies of the MPD, NCIS, and the medical examiner's reports to the defense, the judge, and the jurors. He gave the jurors several minutes to read the reports, knowing that the defense and the judge had already read the reports, and then addressed Hennessey, "I would like these exhibits to be marked prosecution's 1, 2, and 3 and then be entered into the court record."

From the judge, "Does the defense object?"

"No ma'am."

"The exhibits are so entered into the record of this proceeding. You may continue Commander Frisolli."

"I call the medical examiner, Jenny Capice, to the stand."

After the woman was sworn in and took her seat on the witness stand, the prosecutor continued, "Doctor, can you describe the wounds that Lieutenant Pettite suffered at the time of her death?"

The doctor gave her testimony much as it was written in her report, while referring to her notes from time to time. When she was finished, Frisolli asked, "What was the cause of death?"

"Strangulation."

"What did you conclude about the wounds to her neck that was caused by the tool you described as a putty knife?"

"They were done postmortem by the tool that had been honed to a very sharp edge by a very angry killer."

"Objection! The doctor has no way of knowing the state of mind of the killer."

"Sustained. The witness's statement will be stricken from the record. The prosecution may continue."

"Doctor, were you able to establish a time of death?"

"I did a liver temperature test and estimated the time of death to be between 10:00 p.m. and midnight."

The prosecutor was attempting to show that Jimmy had ample time to return to Washington, wait for Nora's return, and then kill her. To the doctor he said, "Thank you doctor. That's all I need from you right now. You may step down."

Before the woman could move, Judge Hennessey addressed her, "Please remain where you are. There may be more questions from the defense." The judge turned to Carol Ann and asked, "Miss Garnett, do you have any questions for this witness?"

"Yes I do. Doctor, you established the time of death between 10:00 p.m. and midnight. Is that correct?"

"Yes, that's what I said."

"Could the death have occurred before or after that time period, say an hour or so either way?"

"Yes. Establishing the time of death is not an exact science. That was my best guess."

"Thank you doctor. That's all I have for you." Carol Ann was confident that the time of death would not help the prosecution and that her objection being sustained indicated that Frisolli had wasted his time with the witness and that he was barking up the wrong tree in building a case against Jimmy.

"Redirect Commander Frisolli?"

"No ma'am."

"Doctor, you are dismissed, subject to recall. Commander Frisolli, call your next witness."

"The prosecution calls Ensign Richard Settie to the stand."

When Settie was sworn in and seated, Frisolli asked, "Will you please describe to the court the events that occurred the night you encountered Corporal Geracollo and Lieutenant Pettite?"

Before Settie began his tale, Carol Ann leaned over toward Jimmy and whispered in his ear, "This could be very interesting. Pay close attention to what he has to say."

Richard gave a well-rehearsed version of the meeting in the restaurant, punctuated with several variations of the actual events.

From Frisolli to Settie, "Why did you involve yourself in the conversation between the corporal and the lieutenant?"

"When I saw Nora at the table, I went over to say hello to her because we had dated in the past."

"Did you know that she was dining with the defendant?"

"No, the man had his back to me as I made my way to the table, and when I reached her, she invited me to sit down."

"What happened when the defendant recognized you?"

"He lost it. He went off on an invective-filled harangue against the Navy, sailors, and me in particular. He threatened to drag me out of the restaurant and beat me unmercifully if I didn't leave immediately."

"What did Lieutenant Pettite do?"

"She told the defendant to calm down and control himself because he was creating a disturbance in the dining room."

"How did he react to her rebuke?"

"He took off on her and threatened her with all kinds of physical abuse if she didn't demand that I leave immediately."

"Did she ask you to leave?"

"No."

"What happened next?"

"Nora demanded that he leave and stated that she didn't want to have anything to do with him anymore. They were finished as a couple."

"Did he leave this time?"

"Yes, but he was red faced, in a rage, and was still ranting as he stormed out of the restaurant."

An objection came from Carol Ann. "He answered the question with yes. Everything after that was commentary and should be stricken from his testimony."

"Overruled. The witness can testify to what he observed."

Frisolli continued, "Did you leave right after the defendant?"

"No. Nora was upset and wanted some time to compose herself, so she suggested that we order coffee."

"Who paid the restaurant bill?"

"I offered to pay it, but she insisted that it was her responsibility and paid the bill."

"Did the two of you leave together?"

"No, Nora wanted some time to herself, so she called for a cab. When I left, she was still sitting alone at the table. That was the last time I saw her."

Carol Ann did not object this time. She just threw it out to the court. "More commentary."

From the bench, "You are out of order counselor. You will get your turn to examine the witness."

Frisolli resumed, "One more question. The medical examiner testified that the defendant's blood was found on the tool embedded in the victim's neck. Is it the same tool that the defendant used to scrape paint on the USS Falcony?"

"It could be. They all look alike."

"Was the paint scrapper ever recovered on the ship?"

"No, it was never turned in, and I never saw it again."

"Was a search conducted to recover the paint scrapper?"

"Yes, the Marines were in charge of searching their own area, but the search found nothing. I wonder why?"

Carol Ann just couldn't help herself as the words fell out of her mouth. "There he goes again."

Judge Hennessey rebuked her. "If you keep doing that, I'll hold you in contempt. If you were in the military, I'd throw you in the brig."

"I apologize to the court. It won't happen again."

After the interruption, Frisolli continued, "Thank you for your testimony, Ensign Settie. I think we all have a clear understanding of the events that led to Lieutenant Pettite's murder."

Carol Ann jumped up out of her chair and was about to say something when Jimmy jerked her back into her seat, while twisting his head and simply saying to her, "No!"

Judge Hennessey interjected, "Commander Frisolli, be careful what you add to the witness's statement, and have your witness stick to the script without any asides. I've warned both sides. If there are any further outbursts, I'll discontinue this court-martial. Do both sides understand what I'm saying?"

Garnett and Frisolli both nodded in the affirmative.

Hennessey continued, "Commander Frisolli, are you finished with this witness?"

"Yes ma'am."

"Miss Garnett, you may cross examine the witness."

Carol Ann moved close to the witness stand, and with a wink at the witness, she asked, "Ensign Settie, you testified that you met Nora Pettite by accident in the restaurant, and that you didn't know who her dinner companion was. Did I understand that correctly?"

"Yes, I didn't know she was there or who she was with."

With a broad smile and a flirting glance, Carol Ann said, "Thank you, Richard. That's very helpful." Settie assumed that defense counsel was enamored with him, which was what she hoped would happen. The man had fallen into the woman's trap. That was his first mistake.

Defense counsel continued, "As the defendant was going through his diatribe, what did you have to say?"

"Very little. I only got in a few words. He controlled the entire conversation and wouldn't tolerate any interruptions."

"Good. Are you sure none of the other diners overheard any of your part of the conversation?"

"I doubt it. I only spoke in very low tones and only a few words."

"I'm glad to hear that. You said that you and Miss Pettite did not leave the restaurant together. Did you offer her a ride home?"

"Yes, but she refused my offer. I told the court that she wanted some time alone, and then she called for a cab."

At this point Carol Ann decided to take a chance and put the witness in a quandary, so she asked, "What taxi company did she call?"

Settie did not expect the question, and he was thrown off guard by it. To him the question seemed inconsequential to his testimony. He hesitated in answering with a coughing fit that lasted several moments. Then he answered, "I don't know. She said it was a local company that she had used before."

What Carol Ann was about to allude to never happened. The gamble could pay off, or it could blow up in her face and give the witness credibility if he did not change his last statement. Her trial experience and instinct told her to go for it, so she said, "Would it interest you to know that I checked with the local taxi companies and none of them reported receiving a phone call from Miss Pettite requesting a pickup, and that some of the restaurant patrons remember the two of you leaving the restaurant together. Would you like to rephrase your answer to the previous question?"

Settie was getting rattled and needed time to compose himself, so he reached over and took a bottle of water from the witness stand and started drinking it slowly. When he had formulated a response, he said, "Now that I'm thinking about it, I may have walked out with her so she could wait for the taxi outside. I drove home alone."

"Is that you final answer?"

"Yes."

"Are you sure?" Carol Ann pushed her luck with another statement she couldn't prove. "Nora wasn't driven away from the restaurant by a taxi."

Frisolli shouted an objection, "She's badgering the witness."

"Sustained. Move on Miss Garnett."

"One last question, Ensign Settie. Did you murder Lieutenant Nora Pettite?"

Settie was shocked by the question. It was the last thing he expected. He shrugged his shoulders in the direction of the prosecutor with an expression that pleaded, "Help me." Frisolli remained stone-faced. His witness was on his own. Richard squirmed in his seat for what seemed an eternity to him and then answered, "No!"

"That's all I have for this witness, ma'am."

As Settie was walking away from the witness stand, it dawned on him that the defense counsel was not his friend. She had led him down a path and then slammed him into a stone wall. He also realized that his house of cards was now on a very shaky foundation.

"Redirect Commander Frisolli?"

"No thank you."

"The prosecution may call its next witness."

"That won't be necessary. The prosecution rests."

"In that case, I believe we've all had enough for one day. We will resume at 9:00 a.m. tomorrow morning. The defense will be on the firing line."

Jimmy and Carol Ann conferred for a few minutes in the empty courtroom. Jimmy started with, "You did to Settie during your cross examination what I wanted to do with my fists. You beat the hell out of him. You did great."

"Thanks, but we're not out of the woods yet. Let's see how we do tomorrow."

Jimmy went back to his cell, and his attorney went back to her office to prepare for the final battle.

Judge Hennessey wasted no time when she entered the courtroom the next morning. She saw that both the prosecution and the defense teams were in place at their tables. She seated herself and announced, "Miss Garnett, call your first witness."

"The defense calls Miriam Bader to the stand."

After Miriam was sworn and seated, Carol Ann began, "Please give your full name, address, and present occupation."

Miriam gave her name and address and concluded with, "I'm a Navy nurse assigned to the Bethesda Naval Hospital."

"You live at the same address as Lieutenant Pettite. Did you know her?"

"Yes, I was her roommate."

"Are you acquainted with Ensign Richard Settie?"

"Yes."

"Please explain to the court how you know Ensign Settie."

"He had dates with Lieutenant Pettite, and he would call for her at our apartment. A couple of times he asked me out on dates."

"Did you go out with him?"

"No."

"Please explain why you didn't date him."

"He was not my type and other personal reasons."

"What personal reasons?"

"I'd rather not answer that question. It might be a violation of Navy regulations."

Commander Frisolli stood and asked the judge, "Is this a fishing expedition? Where is the defense going with this line of questioning?"

Judge Hennessey asked, "Miss Garnett, what is your purpose in asking these questions?"

"I'm setting the foundation for future questions."

"Then do it quickly and move on."

"Miss Bader, did Ensign Settie have occasion to ask you about Nora's personal life?"

"He was always asking me about Nora's personal life. He would call the apartment and ask me what Nora was doing, where she was going, and who she was seeing. It was like he was stalking her. He gave me a creepy feeling."

"Did you answer his questions?"

"I tried not to, but he was very insistent. I'm sure I told him things I shouldn't have, but I just wanted to get rid of him."

"Did you see Ensign Settie on the day Nora died?"

"Yes I did, but I didn't think anything about it until I found out that Nora was murdered."

"What happened on that day?"

"Richard came by the apartment that day looking for Nora. He told me there was an emergency and that he had to find her immediately."

"What did you do?"

"I told him I didn't know where she was."

"How did he react to that statement?"

"He said that she was probably with that Marine and that he had to find them right away."

"How did he know she was seeing a Marine?"

"I don't know. Maybe he saw them together."

"Are you sure you didn't tell him about Nora and the defendant?"

"I may have. I told you, he was always bugging me for information about Nora and who she was seeing. One time I found a post-it with the word 'Marine' and a phone number."

"Did you know that the number you gave to Ensign Settie belonged to the defendant?"

"No. I never met the defendant before today."

"Were you in the habit of going through Nora's personal belongings and sharing the information you found with Ensign Settie?"

"He was threatening and insistent, and I just wanted to get him off my back, so I did what he ordered me to do."

"What happened when you let Richard into the apartment that day?"

"As I said before, he claimed it was an emergency, and then he went into Nora's room and starting rummaging through her things."

"Did he find what he was looking for?"

"I don't know what he was looking for, but when he came out of Nora's room, he had a business card in his hand. He used the apartment phone to call the number on the card and waited for a response."

"Did anyone answer his call?"

"Yes, I heard him ask if Nora Pettite had made a reservation at that restaurant. He must have gotten an answer because he hung up the phone."

"What did he do after the phone call?"

"He said gotcha and left the apartment."

"Thank you, Miriam. Your testimony was very helpful."

"Cross examine Commander Frisolli?"

Frisolli moved to the witness stand and asked, "Do you realize that by giving Ensign Settie Nora's personal information, you may have set in motion a series of steps that eventually led to Nora's murder?"

Carol Ann could have, but did not object, to Frisolli's question for two reasons. Miriam's answer could have pointed to either Jimmy or Richard as the murderer, and she wanted to see where the prosecution was leading the witness.

"I never was strong enough to stop Richard from having his way. I was afraid of him. I loved Nora, and I would never have done anything to hurt her. I regret that I helped Richard. May God help me. Look at what my stupidity led to."

"Did you have a sexual relationship with your roommate?"

"No, not Nora. Never!"

"Did you love Nora?"

"Yes, very much."

"Do you want to see the defendant convicted of her murder?"

Miriam did not have a chance to give her answer to that question because Carol Ann bellowed, "Objection!"

Judge Hennessey did not hesitate. "Sustained." Without pause, she added, "Commander Frisolli, you know better than that. Sit down. Defense, call your next witness."

"The defense calls Gunnery Sergeant Vincent Ascenzio to the stand."

When Vince was sworn and seated, the defense counsel asked, "Are you acquainted with the defendant, James Geracollo?"

"Yes."

"Please explain to the court how you know the defendant."

Vince went through his time with Jimmy from Parris Island, to Camp Lejeune, the voyage on the Falcony, their time together in Iraq, their return to the States with posting to Quantico, and the testing at Bethesda.

"Did you know the defendant was dating Lieutenant Pettite?"

"Every man in the company knew he was seeing someone. It was obvious by the way he acted. I suspected it was Nurse Pettite. I think he fell in love with her the day she treated his wounded hand."

"Was your suspicion ever confirmed?"

"Yes."

"Please explain your confirmation."

Vince explained his meeting with Jimmy on that fateful Saturday night at the bar, and Jimmy's explanation of the events that unfolded in the restaurant between Settie, Nora, and himself.

"You said the defendant was already in the bar when you arrived. What time did the defendant get there?"

"He told me during our conversation that he got there about fifteen minutes before, so I would say about 9:30."

"What time did you meet the defendant in the bar?"

"I would say about 9:45."

"The medical examiner estimated the time of death between 10:00 and midnight. Let's add an hour each way and put the time of death between 9:00 and 1:00 in the morning. Could the defendant have murdered the witness during that time period?"

"Objection!" came from the prosecutor. "The witness has no way of knowing when the victim died."

"Overruled. I want to hear the witness's answer. Gunny, be careful with your answer."

"I don't see how that's possible. Ensign Settie's testimony stated that the defendant left the restaurant before himself and the victim. The drive from the restaurant to the bar would take about a half hour, so if he arrived at the bar at 9:30, then he must have left the restaurant around 9:00. I met him at 9:45. The fifteen minutes in between would not have been enough time for Nora to return to Washington and for Jimmy to drive back to Washington, find Nora, kill her, and then return to the bar."

"What time did you and Jimmy leave the bar?"

"At midnight, when the bar closed."

"Could the defendant have killed the victim between midnight and 1:00 a.m.?"

"That's impossible. We got back to the barracks after twelve. Jimmy went to his area, and I went to mine. I have an office and sleeping quarters in the same building as the defendant. I watched television for a while. Then at 1:00 a.m., I did a bed check, and every man was accounted for, including Jimmy, He was sleeping."

"Poppycock," came from the prosecution table.

Judge Hennessey rapped her gavel and pointed it at the prosecution table while saying, "This is your last warning, Commander Frisolli."

"I apologize, ma'am. I have an overly exuberant assistant at the prosecution table."

"Continue with your examination, Miss Garnett."

"That's all I have for this witness."

Frisolli moved quickly to the witness stand and asked, "Sergeant, you testified that the defendant was sleeping when you did your bed check. Is it possible that you mistook a dummy under the blankets for the defendant?"

"I was not mistaken. I've seen dummies in bed before, and I saw the defendant, not some blowup doll in the bed."

"That's a very descriptive answer, Sergeant. I've never heard it explained that way before. Thank you.

"When you were in Iraq, did anyone ever save your life during combat?"

"I'm sure that happened on more than one occasion. I've been knocked down at times as bullets whizzed over my head. I've had men jump in front of me and take a bullet meant for me."

"Was the defendant one of the men who saved your life?"

The prosecutor's question was intended to demonstrate that Jimmy saved Vince's life in combat and that Vince's testimony was repayment to Jimmy for that action.

Vince answered, "It's possible that my life could have been saved by the defendant, but you must understand what happens in combat. It's mass confusion, and nobody knows the name of the person who did whatever he did to saves lives.

"You're a Navy man, Commander. Let me explain to you something about Marines. Marines are ethically and duty-bound to help one another. You don't have to know the person. Marines take care of Marines, regardless of the situation. It's part of our code. Every Marine knows he can depend on every other Marine in combat. That's the way we survive. It's just the way we are, and we like it that way. I hope that answers your question. I don't know if the defendant ever saved my life, but I do know for a fact that the defendant was sleeping in his bunk when I did the bed check."

"That's all I have for you, Sergeant."

"Redirect Miss Garnett?"

"No ma'am. I think the witness summed up everything very nicely."

"Call your next witness, Miss Garnett."

"The defense rests."

"Commander Frisolli, do you have anything else to offer the court?"

"No ma'am."

"Miss Garnett, do you have any last words for the court?"

"No ma'am."

Judge Hennessey gave her final instructions to the jury panel, ending with, "Gentlemen, you may retire to deliberate."

26

Verdict

After the jury panel had left the courtroom, Judge Hennessey addressed the adversaries, "While the panel is determining a verdict, we should take our lunch break. Be back at 1:00 this afternoon."

When the judge entered the courtroom after the lunch recess, she was surprised to see not only the prosecution and defense in place, but also the jury panel ready to render its verdict.

Seated on the bench, the judge addressed her question to the highest ranking officer on the panel, "Commander, have you reached a verdict?"

"Yes ma'am." The prosecution and the defense stood.

"You may publish it."

"We find the defendant guilty ...." He stopped to clear his throat. "Guilty of fraternization with an officer. He will forfeit a month's pay and a reduction in rank to Lance Corporal."

To the jury the judge said, "Gentlemen, thank you for your service. You are excused." The men left the courtroom. To the opposing parties she said, "Be seated."

She now turned to Frisolli and said, "Commander, I thank you and your assistants for a professional prosecution."

"Thank you, ma'am. We tried to meet our responsibilities during this court-martial."

The judge then turned to the defense and continued, "Thank you, Miss Garnett, for a capable defense. Corporal Geracollo, you are free to go. You may return to your duties, Semper Fi Marine."

Jimmy stood and saluted the judge saying, "Semper Fi ma'am."

Carol Ann and Jimmy sat quietly until the courtroom cleared. Carol Ann stood and started to fill her briefcase with papers. Jimmy was in a daze. He couldn't believe his good fortune, and he didn't know what to do or say, so on impulse he hugged his attorney tightly. When he found his voice and without releasing her, he finally said, "I will never be able to thank you enough for everything you did. You saved my life."

Carol Ann did not break away from Jimmy, and in a soft tone she responded, "You're welcome. I just did my job. I'm happy that you're a free man. Now let me go. This is not seemly courtroom procedure." Jimmy reluctantly released her.

Gunny Ascenzio met Carol Ann and Jimmy outside the courtroom. The lawyer and her client had to return to his place of confinement, the Quantico brig. Carol Ann had court papers for the authorities, and released forms had to be signed. Vince drove Jimmy, and Carol Ann followed in her car.

After the formalities were concluded, Jimmy returned to his cell and retrieved his personal belongings.

Outside the jail, Vince suggested a victory celebration that night and also proposed that they invite Theresa Scafidi to join them so that they could thank her for her help.

Carol Ann nixed that idea by saying, "I don't think we should do that. If we do, she could be accused of orchestrating the court-martial, which she did. If you invite her, you might as well invite the judge and the jury. Let's keep it small. It's over. Better to let sleeping dogs lie."

The three met that night for a quiet dinner with champagne and other assorted alcoholic drinks. As the trio was separating outside the restaurant, Carol Ann said to Vince, "Thanks for your help," and to Jimmy, "keep in touch."

Whenever Jimmy found himself in Washington, which was relatively often by design, Jimmy always made it a point to invite Carol Ann to lunch or dinner. She almost always accepted, and a friendship bloomed.

One might think it strange that sometimes there are positive results from a court-martial, but then again, there are those who still believe in miracles.

The day after Jimmy's court-martial ended, Captain Gregory called his old friend, Marine Corps Captain Boyd Nielsen, who had been a member of the jury panel at Jimmy's trial. When Boyd answered the phone call, Frank asked, "Boyd, how you doing buddy? It's been a long time."

"Is that you, Frank? What's up?"

"I know you were on the jury at the Geracollo court-martial. He's one of my men. What can you tell me about the trial?"

"I don't think we should discuss this over the phone. Let's meet somewhere where we can talk."

The captains met at a small, quiet restaurant outside of Quantico for lunch. They ordered burgers and beers, and then Boyd opened the conversation with, "That court-martial never should have happened. Frisolli had no case, and by the time the defense finished, the prosecution knew it was over and threw in the towel. When the judge sent us to deliberate, we had already made our decision. We sat around munching on sandwiches, drinking coffee, and bullshitting. When the squid commander called for a vote, it was unanimous. Your man never killed the Navy lieutenant, and everybody in the courtroom knew it. If we were forced to find someone guilty of murder, it would have been Ensign Settie. His prosecution testimony was too tight and too well rehearsed. Everybody who has ever watched a television courtroom drama knows that even an honest witness is nervous and will slip up under questioning, no matter how well prepared.

"When we heard Gunny Ascenzio's testimony, we were convinced that Settie's prosecution testimony was fabricated. I'll give him credit though, the man is a good actor and a convincing liar."

"Why didn't you let it go at that, forget the lesser charges?"

"The Navy guys wanted the Marine to pay a penalty for stealing one of their women, so we all agreed on fraternization, a fine, and reduction in rank. Your man got off easy."

Frank came back with, "Some Marines don't always pay attention to good advice. Geracollo was warned that he was skating on thin ice with an officer many times, but he chose to ignore the warning and fell through the ice. The penalty was fair, but the price he paid was more than he could handle."

The friends finished their lunches, and as they separated, Boyd said to Frank, "Keep in touch, Semper Fi."

Part Ten

27

Aftermath

Jimmy was elated with the way the court-martial ended and was comfortable being back among his Marines. The loss of pay was not a problem for him because he was not going anywhere that would require more money than he had to spend, and besides, he remained on the Base where everything he needed was provided for him. For the most part, his duties remained as they were before the trial with a few other responsibilities added because of his lower rank.

The days passed quickly for Jimmy. He kept busy during his work hours, but the nights were a different story. Mostly he was by himself and alone with his thoughts. He missed Nora terribly, and the only thing that relieved his pain was his planning for the future.

Certain future events were set in stone. He would finish his enlistment in the Marine Corps; he would not return to New York; his parents had moved to Florida; he would get a job to support himself; and he would commit himself entirely to carry out successfully his next mission.

The several months left in Jimmy's enlistment passed faster than he had expected, and at the end of the following year, he used his unused leave time to secure an early separation from active duty and became a civilian. He found himself a job as a full-time bartender in a local watering hole not far from the base, and when on the night shift, he often served his comrades from the Iraq campaign.

His regular customers included Claude Jayson, Wally Covence, Nicky B, and of course, his good friend, Vince Ascenzio. On special occasions, Captain Gregory would join a celebration with his men. Jimmy was happy when he could spend some time with his friends, and he tried to treat them well. The bar owner had a firm policy about buybacks, and Jimmy tried to stay within those limits, but whenever the opportunity presented itself, he moved outside the established boundaries. The extra buybacks he gave his buddies was offset by the fewer buybacks he offered to new and irregular customers. Whenever he worked with a cooperative cook, he was able to serve his comrades some complimentary finger food. The bar owner never realized that Jimmy had, in his own way, saddled him with some silent partners.

Outside of working hours, Jimmy spent almost all of his free time in solitary pursuits. He purposely lengthened the time spans between lunches and dinners with Carol Ann. He hoped to disassociate her from himself and his ultimate objective. He did not want her to get entangled in the mess that would follow his failure to secure justice for Nora.

For her part, Carol Ann thought she and Jimmy would spend more, not less, time together when his military service ended, but it was not to be. She hoped that their friendship would rise to a higher level, but that hope was not realized at that time. She noticed that when they were together, Jimmy would have moments when he wandered off their conversation topics, and his mind shifted gears and sent his thoughts into quiet reflection. She worried that something strange and dark was controlling his thinking, and she knew Jimmy would not reveal to her his inner demon. All she could do was worry and pray that whatever was driving him would not destroy him.

Jimmy was forced to spend many hours in planning, preparation, covert surveillance, and record keeping in an effort to achieve success. Everything had to go without a hitch in an exact time frame.

When Jimmy thought the time was right, he went to the bar owner and said, "Boss, I need to take some vacation time. I need to go to Florida. My father is sick."

The boss came back with, "Okay, if you have to go, then go. See if the other bartenders will cover your shifts. What they don't want, I'll hire a sub to fill the rest. Have a good trip. Let me know when you're coming back. Drive safely."

Jimmy spent the next morning and afternoon packing his clothes and personal belongings. He then stowed them in his car. He ate breakfast in his apartment. He walked to a nearby diner for lunch, and at dusk, he had dinner in a local restaurant. After dinner, he walked home, got in his car, and drove away.

The man followed his routine exactly the way he almost always did. He drove from work and arrived at his apartment within the five minute time frame Jimmy had recorded many times. He parked his car and entered his apartment where Jimmy assumed he changed out of his uniform and into running gear. Keeping to his schedule of running every other day, he exited his apartment and started jogging to the park. Jimmy left his concealed position and followed the jogger through the parking lot of the park and out onto the running path. The man stopped to set his timer and pedometer and then started running at a slow pace.

Jimmy was several yards behind the runner and started his run at a slightly faster pace. About a half mile into the run, the path straightened for a long distance. It was dark, but Jimmy could see that there were no other runners in either direction. The road had a woods on its right side and a spreading lawn on its left side. Jimmy knew the time was right to make his move, so he picked up his speed, closed the distance between them, and maintained the man's pace stride for stride.

When he was on the left side of his target, he spoke to the man. "Hi Richard. How are you doing?"

Richard turned his head toward the speaker. At first he didn't recognize the man, but when he did, he started to ask, "What are ...." He never got the rest of the question out of his mouth, and he never saw the right hand punch that slammed into the side of his head and knocked him into the tree line.

Jimmy dragged the dazed and semiconscious man deeper into the trees. Jimmy was sure that no one had seen what happened, but he had to consider other possibilities. If other runners stopped and asked what happened, he would say that his friend had too much to drink and the exertion of running made him puke. In all likelihood, the runners would move on with haste. The other problem was a maintenance worker showing up and asking, "What's going on in the woods?" If that happened, Jimmy would walk out into the open and flash a phony police badge and explain, "My friend is taking a piss." The park worker would hopefully continue on his way at the sight of a police badge.

Fortunately for Jimmy, nobody interrupted his plans. Deep in the trees, Jimmy did what he had planned to do. He would have liked the ordeal to last longer and the suffering to be more intense as he administered justice for Nora, but time was of the essence. With the task completed, he stripped the man naked and placed his clothing and personal belongings in a duffle bag.

He carried the naked man and the duffle bag back to his car, which he had parked earlier in the parking lot. He placed the naked man on a plastic tarp he had placed that afternoon in his trunk. He did not want the man's blood to stain the carpeting in the trunk. He threw the duffle bag into the trunk on top of the victim.

He had one more stop to make before leaving town. His luck held. The parking lot was empty of pedestrians. He stopped next to the dumpster, unlocked the trunk, and removed the lifeless body, which he threw into the trash bin. He slammed the trunk lid closed, got back into the car, and drove away. There were no witnesses.

Jimmy drove through the night for many hours until he neared his objective. He got off the highway and entered Hell Hole Swamp, located in the Francis Marion National Forest in eastern South Carolina. Jimmy seemed to be the only person in the park, and when he found what he was looking for, he stopped atop a bridge. He opened the trunk and took out the duffle bag. He took off his t-shirt and sweatshirt and placed them in the bag, along with the plastic tarp. He filled the duffle bag with heavy stones that he had stored in the trunk. He locked the bag and then threw it off the bridge into the swamp. A group of alligators resting on the shore slid into the swamp and dove for the sinking object. When the gators discovered it was not a meal, they returned to the shoreline and continued their vigil.

Jimmy put on a clean sweatshirt from his clothing in the back of the car and then retraced his route back to the highway and continued his journey. A few miles further on, he found an open diner. At the counter he ordered a large coffee to go, returned to the car, and continued driving south.

In northern Florida, he found a motel with a vacancy and took a room for one night. In the room, he inspected his pants and shoes for blood stains and found none. He went to bed and slept peacefully through the night. In the morning, he ate a hearty breakfast at the motel and then drove to his parents' house in Fort Lauderdale.

28

Alibi

Jimmy arrived at his parents' home in late afternoon. He knocked on the front door, and the door was opened by his mother. The woman was both happy and surprised to see her son, but was at a loss for words, so Jimmy filled in the void with, "Hi mom. How are you doing?"

When his mother found her voice, she answered, "I'm well. How are you doing?"

"I'm good. Aren't you going to invite me in?"

"Of course, come on in."

Jimmy stepped in, and mother and her son hugged and kissed each other. When they separated, she hollered in the direction of the kitchen, where she knew her husband was reading the newspaper. "Antonio, look who's here!"

When Antonio came out of the kitchen and saw his son, he hesitated and then ran full speed ahead and bear hugged his son. The hugging ended after a long moment, and Jimmy's dad said, "What are you doing here? Why didn't you tell us you were coming?"

"I needed a vacation, some sunshine, and warmer weather, so I thought I would do all that by coming to see you, so here I am."

The family sat around the kitchen table drinking coffee and catching up on the latest news. This was the first visit Jimmy had with his parents since he was stationed at the Brooklyn Navy Yard. After Iraq, Jimmy kept in contact with his parents by phone, email, and special occasion cards. They knew about his court-martial and the results, but not the details. He explained everything to them.

Jimmy was starving, and he knew that they enjoyed Early Bird dinners, so he suggested, "Let's go eat dinner."

Marie selected her favorite restaurant, where she and Antonio selected a meal from the prix fixe menu. Jimmy made selections from the standard menu and consumed more food than his parents together. While dining, Marie said to her son, "What happened to your hand? It's all swollen?"

Jimmy was hoping his injury would go unnoticed by his parents, but they would have to be blind not to notice, so he responded, "It looks worse than it is. I was rolling a keg of beer into place at the bar, and it got away from me and pinned my hand against the wall. It's a little swollen, but it should be alright in a day or two."

In a motherly fashion, Marie followed up with, "It looks worse than swollen. You should have a doctor look at it."

The rest of the meal passed without any further references to his injured hand.

Jimmy might have been able to fool his parents and appease his mother, but he could not deceive himself. His hand hurt like hell, and he knew he had broken bones in his hand from repeatedly punching Richard in the head until his skull fractured and dug into his brain.

The next morning at breakfast, Jimmy saw an opportunity to get medical aid, so he said to his father, "I see you're replacing some shingles on the roof. I'll help you finish the job today."

Father and son were on the roof replacing shingles. Jimmy carried the new shingles onto the roof and put them in place while Antonio nailed them down. Jimmy saw his chance when he noticed that his father was nailing by rote. It was a conditioned reflex. He could hit the nails on the head without actually looking at them. Jimmy put his hand over a nail, and Antonio swung his hammer down on his son's hand.

The pain was agony, but Jimmy did not cry out. He simply started shaking his arm, trying to dispel the pain in his hand.

Antonio went ashen when he saw what he had done and exclaimed, "I'm sorry. I wasn't looking at what I was doing. Are you okay?"

"It hurts, but I don't think you did any damage. Let's finish this job, and then I'll take a look at it." They finished the roofing job and then put their tools away.

Jimmy noticed that the nail had punctured his hand while he was washing up. He said to his mother, "I think I'll take your advice and see a doctor. This hole may need a tetanus shot."

Jimmy drove himself to a nearby walk-in Immediate Medical Care Center and signed in. He waited while the doctor saw three other patients, and then it was his turn.

The doctor examined the swollen hand with the puncture wound. He cleaned the wound and gave Jimmy a shot of penicillin for protection. The doctor took some x-rays, and while he was reading them, he asked, "What happened to your hand?"

Jimmy explained about the roofing accident, but the doctor wasn't about to accept that explanation, so he stated, "One hammer blow couldn't cause this kind of damage unless the hammer weighed fifty pounds." Jimmy wasn't caught off guard, so he retold the story about the rolling beer keg.

The doctor was still suspicious because he noticed multiple bone fractures and bone chips. Some of the bones had started to knit themselves. He put a soft cast on the broken hand and gave Jimmy prescriptions for pain killers. Jimmy did not fill the scripts because he wanted the pain to be a reminder of what he had done. Each reminder brought a smile to his face.

Jimmy spent the next two days following his parent's itinerary: breakfast at home, a trip to the beach to bask in the sun for a few hours, shopping (his mother loved to shop even when she didn't buy anything except groceries), Early Bird dinners, and watching television. There was constant conversation.

On the day after the roofing accident, Jimmy picked up a copy of the Lauderdale Herald Times while sipping his third cup of coffee. In the National News section, he saw an article that was picked up off a wire service. The article was a recap of a Washington Tribune posting. Jimmy folded the paper and placed it on the breakfast table, finished his cup of coffee, and then went to his room and logged onto his computer.

He had no trouble finding what he was looking for, and when it popped up on the screen, he read the caption:

Unidentified Naked Body Found Behind Bethesda Hospital

Jimmy did not read the details of the story because he knew what they were. He had been there.

The next morning after breakfast, Jimmy announced to his parents, "I think it's time for me to move on. I've enjoyed the rest and relaxation."

From his mother, "Why don't you stay a few more days and let your hand heal up. Can you drive with that hand?"

"Mom, my hand feels good. If I stay here any longer, I'll turn into a lazy bum. I have to get back to work. I need the money."

Jimmy went to his room, packed his belongings, and then loaded his bags in the car. After emotional and tear-filled goodbyes, he got in his car and headed back to the scene of the crime.

29

Investigation

The hospital worker was about to throw the trash in the bin when she noticed the naked body. She took out her cell phone and started dialing 911, but stopped and cancelled the call. She remembered Tyrone's story of finding a dead body in the dumpster and the lengthy interrogation by the police. Tyrone ended his tale with, "A lot of bullshit questions from the cops; a waste of my time."

Nina was no fool. She didn't have time to waste with cops, so she left the garbage bags on the ground and went back into the hospital. Using the phone in an empty office, she dialed 911.

The 911 operator asked, "What is your emergency?"

"There's a dead body in the garbage container behind Bethesda Hospital."

"Stay on the line. I'll get back to you after I notify the police."

Nina hung up the phone and left the empty office with the door closed behind her. As she returned to the kitchen, she justified her action by thinking, "This is a situation for police involvement; not involvement by a cafeteria worker."

Officer Tommy Gordon drove his patrol car into the lot behind the hospital and saw a dumpster with some garbage bags on the ground next to it. He assumed that was the crime scene, so he drove over and parked his car next to the garbage bags. He got out of the police vehicle and looked into the dumpster. Sure enough, there was a dead body inside. He looked around for the 911 caller, but found no one.

He called the precinct desk sergeant and reported his finding. The sergeant told him to remain where he was and to tape off the crime scene. Although Tommy didn't need the reminder, the sergeant added, "Keep the spectators away and don't let anyone touch anything."

Detective Tommy Garlin and Medical Examiner Jenny Capice arrived within a few minutes of each other and went to work. The detective did a cursory inspection of the body and the contents of the container, but he found no ID or anything that might be evidence connected to the crime. The medical examiner did a visual inspection of the body and commented, "This guy looks like he went fifteen rounds with Ali with no gloves."

The doctor asked the detective to remove the body from the container and place it on the ground so she could continue her examination. The detective and the policeman raised the body out of its resting place and placed it on a tarp on the ground.

Capice continued her examination, and the detective began to go through the garbage. As Tommy went through the different layers of waste, he threw the inspected refuse out of the box onto the ground. When he was finished, he tried to wipe the remains of the garbage off his suit. He had some success with the solid objects, but he could not dispel the stench that clung to his clothes.

Garlin went over to Capice and asked, "What did you find, Doctor? How long has he been in there?"

"My tests indicate that he's been dead nine to twelve hours. It looks like he's been beaten to death. Whoever did this wasn't fooling around. He must have been a powerful man. This was personal. I believe you have a murder on your hands, Detective. Did you find an ID for the victim?"

"Nothing. Whoever did this planned it very carefully. From the looks of the victim, I'd say the victim and the killer had a history."

Jenny and Tommy had worked many cases together and had developed a professional relationship over the years. They knew how to contact each other and shared information on their cases. Jenny called the morgue for a pickup and then said to Tom, "I'll try to identify this guy when I do the autopsy, and then I'll call you."

"Thanks Jenny. I appreciate the heads up. Talk to you later. Let's get together some day for a few drinks."

The next morning, Jenny called Tom and reported, "ID'd the victim through his fingerprints. He was in the system. He's a Navy

Ensign named Richard Settie. He's stationed at the Pentagon. He was definitely beaten to death, and it looks like he was kicked or punched or both until his skull was fractured and pierced his brain. I didn't find any evidence that any weapons or heavy objects were used by the killer to inflict the injuries. If the killer did this with his fists, he must have broken his hand as a result."

"Thanks Jenny. I'll notify NCIS. Maybe they can figure out who's involved in what happened. Got anything else for me?"

"It may be a coincidence, but didn't we handle a case together a year or so ago where we found a dead, naked Navy nurse in the same dumpster behind the same hospital."

"That's right. I forgot all about that case. I wonder if the two cases are connected. I'll keep you in the loop."

After reviewing his past cases, detective Garlin called NCIS Agent Lou Worthy and offered, "I've got another one for you." He went on to apprise Lou of the reason for his call and explained what details he had of Ensign Settie's death.

Before ending the call, Tom asked Lou, "Do you remember the case of a dead Navy nurse we worked together about a year ago?"

"Vaguely. Why do you ask?"

"What happened with that case?"

"We never solved that case. The military followed up with a court-martial, but the guy got off on the murder charge. Court-martials are way above my pay grade. What about it?"

"Do you think there's a connection between the nurse's death and this guy Settie? They were both in the Navy."

"I'll keep that in mind during our investigation. Thanks for calling. I'll let you know if we find anything."

That was the beginning of the investigation into the death of Ensign Richard Settie by the MPD and NCIS.

The Navy interviewed everybody connected with Settie's professional and personal life and came up empty handed. The Navy Brass decided that the killer must be a civilian, so they stopped investigating and turned the case over to the MPD. The Navy's involvement in the outcome of the case did not end with the end of its investigation.

30

Political Pressure

Detective Garlin was called down to the office of the police commissioner, John Burkes. Tommy, his mind occupied with concerns of what the commissioner wanted from him, sat outside the commissioner's office awaiting the meeting with his lordship. When he was called into the inner sanctum, the commissioner commanded, "Sit down, Tom. Do you need anything; coffee, water, soda, a shot?"

"No sir. Thank you."

"Tom, you're the lead detective on the Settie case. How's it going?"

"Very slowly. There was no evidence found at the crime scene that could lead us to the killer. No witnesses have come forward, and I have no suspects. It's almost like it is the perfect crime."

"There's a pain in the ass under secretary of the Navy named Rex Roberts who keeps calling the mayor and busts his balls because we haven't solved Settie's murder yet. The mayor is all over my ass and the ass of the district attorney. The mayor wants the case solved, and he doesn't care how you do it or who gets hurt in the process. Just put someone on trial or in the grave and close this case. Remember, shit flows downhill, and right now it's flowing down from the mayor over me and the DA. Don't let it land on your retirement plans. I've told your bosses to give you everything you need to bring this case to a satisfactory conclusion. Don't let me down. Now go and make everybody happy. Thanks for coming in, Tommy."

Detective Garlin called District Attorney Jake Bauman, who had called the detective to testify on the witness stand on many occasions. Tommy started the conversation with, "I just came from the police commissioner's office, and it looks like we'll be working together again shoveling shit against the tide. I've got nothing on the Settie case. Got any suggestions to get me started?"

"I'm glad you called, Tom. You're right, we're up against the wall on this one. Time is not on our side. That asshole under secretary, Roberts, calls me every day. He wants the case solved yesterday. He doesn't care if I indict the president so long as someone goes on trial. Whoever killed Settie must have known him pretty well. I'd start with the nurse's boyfriend."

Since the detective had no place else to start, he decided to take the district attorney's advice.

Garlin found out where Jimmy worked and who owned the bar, so he decided to talk to the boss first in order to get some background information on Jimmy. He made an appointment to meet the owner at his home. The owner invited the detective into his home, and when the two men were seated, he asked, "Can I give you some refreshment?"

"No thanks. Maybe later. What can you tell me about your bartender, Jimmy Geracollo?"

The owner told Tommy how Jimmy came to be his employee and then asked, "Is Jimmy in trouble?"

"No, this is just some routine questions we cops go through. I assume you know about the death of Ensign Settie. It was all over the newspaper and television. It seems that he and Geracollo were dating the same nurse who was murdered about a year ago. One thing may have nothing to do with the other. I'm just checking it out."

Tommy gave the bar owner the date of Settie's death and then asked, "Was Geracollo working at the bar that night?"

"No. That was the first day of his vacation. He was going to Florida to visit his sick father."

"Thanks. That about covers it." Tommy left the owner's house.

When Tommy got back in his car, he took out his cell phone and dialed Geracollo's phone number. When Jimmy answered his phone, the detective introduced himself. "I'm detective Garlin of the MPD," then added, "I'd like to speak with you about a case I'm working on. Is that okay with you?"

Jimmy asked, "What case are you working on?"

"I'd like to tell you that in person. Can I stop by your place so we can discuss the case?"

"I'm okay with that. Do you have my address?"

"Yes I do. I'll see you in a few minutes."

When Tommy knocked on Jimmy's apartment door, he was admitted without delay and offered a seat. Introductions were made, and then Jimmy asked, "Can I offer you something to drink?"

"No thank you. I've already had enough coffee for one day." Tommy explained the reason for his visit, saying, "I'm investigating the death of Ensign Richard Settie, and I understand you two had a confrontation the night Nora Pettite was murdered."

"The confrontation started long before that night. What has his death got to do with her death? Am I a suspect?"

"No, no, nothing like that. You knew both victims, and I was hoping that you might know something that could help me with my investigation."

"Sorry, but I had nothing to do with that man after Nora died."

"One more question. Where were you the night Settie died?"

"On my way to Florida."

"What time did you leave for Florida?"

"After I ate dinner and the traffic died down."

"I was hoping to learn more, but if that all you got, I'll be leaving. Thanks for seeing me." Tommy gave Jimmy his business card and said, "If you can think of anything else that might help me, give me a ring." Then the detective left.

Jimmy did not want the detective to see his injured hand because it might raise questions that he did not want to answer, so he removed the soft cast and then noticed that much of the swelling had gone, which was a relief. During the interview with the detective, Jimmy kept his right hand in his pocket.

Tommy never did see the injured hand, but his policeman's instinct made him wonder about the cover up.

Detective Garlin walked into his boss's office the next day and asked for permission to travel to Florida to interview Jimmy's parents and maybe even uncover the mystery of the hidden hand. After an extensive Q and A with his boss, Tommy was given permission to take the trip.

31

On the Road

The next morning, detective Garlin started his drive to Florida. He set his odometer to zero and noted his starting time. He wanted to determine how long the trip was and how many hours it would take to reach his destination.

He stopped for a quick lunch in South Carolina and had dinner at a motel where he was staying overnight in Florida. He had breakfast at the same motel and then set out on the rest of his journey. He arrived at Fort Lauderdale in early afternoon.

His doorbell ring was answered by Mrs. Geracollo, and when she opened the door, he introduced himself and explained the reason for his visit and the basics of the case he was working on. Marie invited him in and then called to her husband, "Antonio, come in here and join us."

The three of them were seated around a coffee table in the living room when Antonio asked, "Do you think my son is responsible for the death of that sailor?"

"He is not a suspect in the murder at this time. He is what we call a person of interest because he had a history with the deceased. With your help, I can cross his name off the list of possible suspects."

Garlin went through his lists of questions and wrote down the responses he received.

"What time did your son arrive at your home?"

Marie answered, "In late afternoon."

"What was the reason for his visit?"

Marie explained, "He needed a vacation, wanted some sun and warm weather, so he decided to visit us."

The detective decided to take a gamble at this point, so he asked, "Did your son injure his hand while he was here?"

Antonio answered, "Yes," and then went on to explain the roofing accident.

Another gamble, "Was your son's hand injured before the roofing accident?"

Antonio had an inkling of where the detective's questioning was going and was about to say "No" when Marie beat him to the punch, "His hand didn't look injured, but it was very swollen."

"Did he explain why his hand was swollen?"

From Marie, "He said he had an accident at work, something about a rolling beer keg. I told him to see a doctor."

"Did he go to the doctor?"

Antonio got back into the questioning, "Yes, after the roofing accident. I'll give you the doctor's card."

Tommy had the feeling that Antonio was getting suspicious about his line of questions and their intent, so he folded his notebook and said, "I think that is all I need from you. Thanks for your help." He placed his business card with his contact information on the table and added, "If you think of anything else that may be helpful, call me. Thanks for inviting me into your home."

When Tommy left the house, Antonio called his son and told him the details of the detective's visit.

Tommy put the address of the clinic into his GPS and followed the directions to his next stop.

When he entered the clinic, he went to the receptionist's desk, handed the doctor's card to the woman sitting behind the desk, and asked, "Is this doctor on duty today. I'd like to speak to him."

"Yes, the doctor is here, but you'll have to wait your turn. Please be seated."

Tommy flashed his badge and said, "Police business. I don't have time to wait."

"I'll see what I can do."

The receptionist led Tommy to the doctor's office and said, "Take a seat. The doctor will be with you shortly."

When the doctor came into the office, introductions were made, and then the detective began the interview, "Doctor, do you remember a patient you treated some time ago named James Geracollo?"

"Yes. What about him?"

"Can you describe his injuries?"

"His records are confidential."

"I know they are, but I'm investigating a murder, and I need the information in those records. I could get a court order, but that would be a waste of a lot of time. Can you help me?"

"Does the patient know you're here?"

"I'm sure he does by now."

"In that case, I'll call him and ask if I can release his information to you."

The doctor went into another room and made a call to Jimmy. When he returned to his office, he announced, "Mr. Geracollo said it's okay for me to talk to you. He said he always likes to cooperate with the authorities."

The doctor retrieved Jimmy's file and explained his examination, X rays, and the medical treatment he gave to the patient.

When the doctor finished his report, the detective asked, "Was the swelling in his hand the result of the hammer blow?"

"No way. The bones were broken and had begun to heal. The injury to the hand happened before the roofing accident."

"In your professional judgment, what caused the damage to the injured hand?"

"Hard to say. It could have happened under any of a hundred situations. My best guess, and it's a guess, is that the patient used his fist as a battering ram."

"Thank you, Doctor. That's all I need at the moment. If anything comes of this case, we may have to subpoena your records."

Detective Garlin left the doctor's office, got in his car, and started the return trip to Washington.

Part Eleven

32

Déjà Vu

The morning after detective Garlin returned from Florida, he called District Attorney Bauman, and when his call was answered, he addressed his friend, "Jake, I just got back from Florida, and I have some information that might help you with the Settie case." Tommy went on to enumerate what he had learned from Jimmy, Jimmy's boss, the Geracollos, and the doctor who treated Jimmy's injured hand.

After the phone call, DA Bauman tallied the pros and cons of seeking an indictment against Geracollo for the murder of Settie. The pros were nonexistent: the Navy's investigation led to nothing of value; there was not a single witness to the murder; there was no list of viable suspects; and the only reason Geracollo was considered was because of his relationship with the deceased Nora Pettite, his confrontation with Settie, and his court-martial for the Pettite murder. The cons against indictment would fill a chapter in a law book because of the absence of pros, so a non-indictment seemed the best cause of action.

But with Roberts and the mayor breathing down his neck, the DA decided to reject the obvious course of action and consider other avenues of pursuit to save his job.

Bauman considered the information he had that might turn the tide in favor of indictment. What he had was a list of suspicions, conjectures, and weak circumstantial evidence, but he recalled that in the past, crafty lawyers had won cases with much less in their favor.

The district attorney's survival was on the line, so he called detective Garlin and ordered him to arrest James Geracollo for the murder of Ensign Richard Settie.

The first hurdle in convicting a person accused of a crime was to secure an indictment against that person. It was a commonly accepted belief in the justice system that a competent prosecutor could convince a grand jury to indict the proverbial ham sandwich. Jake was confident he could secure an indictment with the presentation of guesswork in the guise of evidence, so he presented his case to the grand jury.

District Attorney Bauman called detective Garlin as his first witness, and through skillful questioning and interpretation of the detectives answers, he was able to stress that the accused was the only possible murderer of the deceased. He highlighted the contradictory statements made to the detective by the accused, the bar owner, the parents of the accused, and the doctor who treated him. Jimmy told his boss that he was going to Florida to visit his sick father, but he told his parents that he needed a vacation, so he came to visit them. Jimmy claimed he injured his hand in the beer barrel and roofing accidents, but his explanations were dismissed by the doctor who treated his hand injury.

Bauman even allowed the detective to theorize about a discrepancy in the travel time of his trip to Florida and that of Jimmy's. The detective calculated that Jimmy should have arrived at his parents' home a few hours earlier than he did if he left at the time he claimed. After that testimony, Bauman turned to the jurors and speculated, "I wonder what occurred during those missing hours?"

Jimmy was the next witness to be called, and it should be pointed out to the reader that according to the grand jury rules, Jimmy was not allowed to have his lawyer present for consultation or advice. The DA asked Jimmy several questions, which he answered with the same statements that detective Garlin had attributed to him during his testimony. Jimmy did not deviate from his prepared responses. When he was finished, he was excused and left the room. It would be up to the jurors to believe him or not.

The district attorney called only those two witnesses to present his case, and then he gave his final instruction to the jurors and they retired to deliberate. Three hours later, the grand jury returned a true bill of indictment. James Geracollo would go on trial for the murder of Ensign Richard Settie.

Jimmy appeared in court with his lawyer and was charged with murder. A bail hearing followed the charge. The DA asked the judge to confine Jimmy during the course of the trial, and his lawyer pleaded for ROR (Released on Your Own Recognizance).

The judge had read the grand jury report and concluded that the DA would have a tough row to hoe if he was going to get a conviction with the lack of evidence he had, so the judge granted ROR.

33

Pre Trial Preparations

When Jimmy returned to his apartment after the court hearing, he found Vince and Carol Ann sitting in his living room. His surprise moved him to ask, "What are you two doing here?"

"We came to save your ass from death row," answered Vince. He then asked, "Why didn't you tell us you were in trouble?"

"I did not want to get anyone else involved in this. It was all my own doing, and I have to handle it by myself."

Carol Ann stood and said her peace. "I should be mad at you for not calling me, but I'm not. I want to help you get out of this mess. By the way, where did you get that dumb ass lawyer who represented you in court? He should have argued that the charges be dropped."

"He was recommended to me. I thought he did a good job. He got me ROR."

"A first year law student could have done that. I'm going to call that guy and tell him his services are no longer needed. I hope you didn't give him too much money up front. From now on I'm your lawyer."

"I owe him money. I'll pay him what I owe him, and you can be my lawyer, although I didn't want you to get involved."

"You don't know what's good for you, and I've always been involved with you since day one."

Vince Ascenzio didn't come to this meeting to referee the different analyses of the current situation, so he broke into their conversation. "Now is not the time for you two to be arguing with each other. We have to figure out how to win this trial."

Carol Ann took the lead. "Alright, let's look at the evidence. The only reason the bail judge granted ROR was because he knew that the DA had at best a very weak case, and at worst a non-existent case. From my point of view, the DA has only incidental connections between Jimmy and the murder, nothing solid.

"I don't understand why he's taking this case to trial. It's a case he must know he has very little chance of winning. Everything in his past indicates that he shouldn't have touched this case with a ten foot pole. There must be something going on here that only he knows about."

Jimmy asked, "Is there any way to find out why he's doing this to me? Why would he risk his reputation on a case he can't win?"

"I doubt it. Whatever is driving him is something he's keeping to himself. Whatever it is it must be something very powerful to make him take a chance like this. Once he went to the grand jury, there was no turning back. He's all in."

"So what do we do now," came from Vince.

"We prepare for trial the same way we prepared for the court-martial. We strengthen our arguments and line up our witnesses."

Jimmy asked, "Can Bauman use anything from my court-martial to hurt me during the trial?"

"I'm sure he'll bring in your confrontation with Settie the night Nora was killed. He'll try to imply that you killed Settie because you were convinced that he killed Nora. It's a stretch, but you're the only link to Settie and Nora."

"Do you want me to explain to you what happened the night Settie died?"

"It doesn't matter what happened to him that night. The only thing I needed to know was that you were driving to Florida that night to visit your parents."

Vince came back into the conversation. "Something has always bothered me about Nora's death. Who had Jimmy's paint scrapper that ended up in her neck?"

From Jimmy, "It had to be someone on the Falcony, and the only one on that ship who would have a reason to keep the scrapper was Settie so he could frame me for Nora's murder when we wouldn't end our relationship, and he decided to kill her."

Vince asked Carol Ann, "Is there any way we can use the paint scrapper to our advantage at trial?"

The lawyer answered, "I don't see how. The only evidence found on the paint scrapper was Jimmy's and Nora's blood."

Vince bolted out of his chair and headed for the door, but before he could make his escape, Jimmy yelled at him, "Where are you going?"

"I just thought of something that might help us."

Vince got in his car and went in search of Nicky B.

34

The Judge

The scheduling judge assigned the Geracollo case to Carolyn Belowski because she had a reputation for fairness and did not tolerate any nonsense in her courtroom. All of the judges in the courthouse were hoping to avoid the Geracollo case because, although it appeared on the surface like a slam dunk winner for the defense, there were no predictable outcomes for any jury trial, and this kind of trial might be full of surprises and blow up in someone's face. Judge Belowski got the case because the chief judge was convinced that she was the one best able to control an explosive courtroom.

Judge Belowski's policy was to invite the opposing parties of a trial to meet with her so she could explain her ground rules for the conduct of those participating in her courtroom.

Both parties agreed to meet with the judge at a specified date and time, and that date was kept. Carol Ann and Jake appeared in the judge's office.

The judge introduced herself to Carol Ann and nodded to Jake, who had met her many times before that day. The adversaries greeted each other. When the formalities were concluded, the judge opened the meeting, "I asked you here to establish the procedures for this trial. Mr. Bauman has appeared in my court before, so I'm sure he's familiar with my rules, but I believe, Miss Garnett, that this will be your first time in my courtroom. Do you have any concerns before I continue?"

Carol Ann didn't waste any time getting to her point. "Your Honor, you can save the court a lot of time if you dismiss the charges against my client now. Mr. Bauman has nothing that connects my client to the murder of Mr. Settie. This trial will be a sham and an embarrassment to the justice system."

Judge Belowski was no fool, and she was well informed about why District Attorney Bauman wanted to continue with this trial; the Navy and the mayor were breathing down his neck. Dismissing this case could be justified on legal precedence, but if she did dismiss the charges at this time, the anger and fallout from her decision would shift from the district attorney to her. With those consequences in mind, she responded to Carol Ann's request with, "It is my policy to allow a trial to go to conclusion and allow the jury to make the final determination of guilt or innocence."

Carol Ann was about to continue her argument with the judge, but then thought better of the idea and said to the judge, "I had to ask."

"I understand that you have to act in the best interest of your client. I would expect nothing less from you."

"Are there any other requests from either of you before I continue?"

Neither side made any statement or asked any questions.

The judge continued, "I suspect this trial will be a short one, possibly a few days." Looking directly at the DA, she said, "When questioning a witness, I don't want you to go on a fishing trip with hearsay, opinion, or showmanship. Keep it simple with questions and answers; no discourse. Let's try to avoid a lot of objections and parlays with me at the bench. Exchange your witness lists and stick to them.

"I expect both of you to act in a professional manner. I don't want you to put on a performance for the jury, the spectators, or the media. This is a trial, not a television show.

"Once a trial date is set, I will be very reluctant to grant any delays, postponements, or continuances except under extremely extraordinary circumstances. Have you two discussed a plea deal, or do you intend to?"

A collective "No" was the response.

Knowing that the district attorney had a very weak case, the judge feared that he might opt for a dismissal of the charges against the defendant during trial if things were going badly for him. A dismissal at that time would allow the DA to avoid the embarrassment of a loss, and he would be able to recharge the defendant at some time in the future.

To the judge, a dismissal during a trial was not only a waste of her time, but that of the court's and the defense and a waste of taxpayer's money, so she said to the prosecutor, "Mr. Bauman, I want you to understand that once the first witness takes the stand, jeopardy is attached, and the jury will decide a verdict."

DA Bauman understood the judge's concern, so he nodded in the affirmative. He did not want the final decision to come from him.

The judge proposed a trial date, and it was accepted by both sides. The trial would start in three weeks.

35

The Trial

On the date set for the start of the trial at 9:00 a.m., Judge Belowski walked out of her chambers and took her seat on the bench. She was happy to see that both the prosecution and defense were seated at their tables, and she welcomed them and those assembled in the courtroom with, "Good morning. Let's get started. Mr. Bauman, call your first witness."

Bauman stood and addressed the judge, "Your Honor, before I call my first witness, I would like to enter into the court record the testimony of Ensign Richard Settie given at the court-martial of the defendant, James Geracollo."

Garnett jumped out of her chair and shouted, "Objection! What happened at the court-martial has nothing to do with this trial!"

The judge thought to herself, "Oh no, we're only a few minutes into this trial, and already there's an objection." But she was quick to react and asked, "Mr. Bauman, do you have an answer for the defense's objection?"

"Since Mr. Settie cannot be here to speak for himself, I will be referring to his sworn testimony during this trial to bring certain relevant information to the attention of the jury."

"The objection is overruled. I'll allow it. Continue with your witness, Mr. Bauman."

"I call as my first witness Detective Garlin of the Metropolitan Police Department."

After the detective was sworn in and seated, the prosecutor started his examination. "The deceased, Mr. Richard Settie, swore at the court-martial of the defendant that he and the defendant argued at a restaurant on the night that Nora Pettite was murdered.

During your investigation, were you able to confirm that the two argued that night?"

"Yes, the defendant told me that they argued and that their disagreement started before their confrontation that night."

"The defendant is on trial for the murder of Mr. Settie. Did you know that he was also court-martialed for the murder of Lieutenant Pettite?"

"Yes, it was in the files I reviewed."

"Objection! What has that trial got to do with this trial of my client, who was exonerated of that charge?"

"Where are you going with this, Mr. Bauman?" asked the judge.

"I want the jury to understand that the defendant has a history of being charged with the murder of Navy personnel."

"The objection is sustained. The question and answer will be stricken from the record. Be careful, Mr. Bauman. Don't stray too far afield."

"Did the defendant provide an alibi for the night of the Settie murder?"

"Yes he did."

"Please explain to the court the nature of his alibi."

Detective Garlin went on to describe Jimmy's explanation of his whereabouts on the night of the murder, that he was on his trip to Florida to see his parents.

"Did you accept his alibi as truthful and accurate?"

"I accepted the fact that the trip took place, but my follow up investigation uncovered some contradictions in the defendant's statements and those of others."

"Objection! The detective is not a mind reader. He can't know which statements are factual and which are contradictory or fiction."

Judge Belowski was getting frustrated with the defense's objections. She felt that if this course of action kept coming up, the trial would go on forever, so she asked the defense counsel, "Miss Garnett, do you plan to object to every statement given by this witness?"

"No, Your Honor, only those statements that are objectionable."

The judge continued, "The witness is an experienced investigator and can often separate fact from fiction. The jury should hear what he had learned during his investigation. The objection is overruled. The witness may continue with his testimony."

The prosecutor asked, "Detective, can you describe to the court the contradictions you encountered during your investigation?"

Referring to his notes from time to time, the detective itemized the statements made by the bar owner, the Geracollos, and the doctor that did not agree with the statements made by the defendant. The only thing that was not in doubt was the fact that Jimmy took the trip to Florida.

"Based on your trip to Florida, did you discover any other discrepancies between your trip and that of the defendant?"

"I calculated that there were a few missing hours in the defendant's description of the trip."

"Objection! If a hundred people took that same trip, there would be hundreds of discrepancies in their descriptions."

"The detective is entitled to raise the possibility of a time difference in their trips. Defense counsel will have the opportunity to cross examine the witness. The objection is overruled. Continue Mr. Bauman."

The prosecutor turned to face the jury, and as he had before the grand jury, he opined, "I wonder what happened during those missing hours?"

An exasperated Carol Ann pleaded with the judge, "Your Honor, please."

The judge admonished the prosecutor. "Keep your comments to yourself, Mr. Bauman. Now continue with this witness."

"That's all I have for this witness."

The judge gave her next instruction. "The defense may cross examine the witness."

"Detective, is it possible that your calculation of the missing hours could be explained away by other circumstances that you failed to consider?"

"I suppose so."

"I'll take that as a yes."

"Could your supposed contradictions be reconciled by other factors such as faulty recollection, yes or no?"

"Yes, some of them, but not all of them."

"Your Honor, the witness answered 'Yes' to the question and then added some commentary on his answer. His commentary should be stricken from the record."

"I agree." The judge addressed the court stenographer, "Strike the last part of the witness's statement. Continue with your cross examination, Miss Garnett."

"Detective Garlin, how many suspects other than the defendant did you investigate for the murder of Ensign Settie?"

"None. The defendant was the only one investigated."

"That's all I have for this witness, Your Honor."

From the bench, "Redirect Mr. Bauman?"

"No, Your Honor."

The judge continued, "The witness is excused subject to recall. Mr. Bauman, call your next witness."

"That's all I have, Your Honor. I rest my case."

Judge Belowski decided to take a break at that time, so she said to the courtroom, "In that case, I think we could all use a short recess. We will reconvene in thirty minutes."

When the recess ended, both the defense and the prosecution were prepared to continue the trial, so the judge announced, "Miss Garnett, it's your turn at bat. Call your first witness."

"I call Doctor Victor Conte to the stand."

"Detective Garlin has asserted that there was a contradiction in the defendant's account of how he injured his hand and the doctor's contention that the injury could not have happened as a result of the beer keg and the roofing accidents. What is your professional opinion as to the cause of the injury?"

"I am aware of the defendant's statement and the conversation between the detective and the treating doctor. I have read the doctor's report of his findings and treatment. The doctor may not be aware of it, but the standard half keg full of beer weighs 160 pounds. If the defendant's hand was crushed by the weight of the keg, he could have suffered the kind of injury he claimed. He was lucky the injury wasn't worse. In my opinion, the defendant's statement could be truthful."

"Thank you Doctor for your testimony. I'm sure the jury now understands how the defendant injured his hand."

"Cross examine, Mr. Bauman?"

"Doctor Conte, are you being paid by the defense for your testimony today?"

"Yes, I received the standard fee."

"No more questions for this witness."

The judge addressed the defense counsel. "Miss Garnett, it is getting near the lunch break. Would you like to call your next witness after the break?"

Carol Ann knew what was going to happen with the next witness, and she wanted to get through it today because she had another surprise in store for tomorrow, so she answered, "No, Your Honor, I would like to get through the next witness before the break."

"Fine. Call your next witness."

Vincent Ascenzio was called and took the oath. "I swear to tell the truth, the whole truth, and nothing but the truth," then he added, "as I understand it."

Bauman was out of his seat in seconds, in a rage, and asked, "Your Honor, what is going on here? The witness is out of order."

Judge Belowski didn't hesitate. "Both sides, in my chambers now! You too Mr. Ascenzio."

With everyone seated in her chambers, the judge said to Vince, "Explain yourself, Mr. Ascenzio."

"The way I see it, we live in a world where there are many variations of the truth. In this day and age, truth is relative and not absolute. In other words, truth is in the mind of the beholder and is determined by the beholder's interpretation of events.

"We live in a country where the president on many, many occasions promises the people certain things, knowing full well that he will not deliver on those promises, and that he is patently lying to achieve a desired outcome. It happens so often that eventually the lies become acceptable behavior.

"The highest court in the land takes perfectly clear words in our laws that our lawmakers wrote, and the judges turn those words on their heads and give a new interpretation to those words that negates the true meaning of the original words and creates a false conclusion.

"Country-wide polls indicate that a large majority of the citizenry believe our elected representatives are chronic liars and thieves only interested in their own betterment, and yet at election time, ninety percent of these liars are returned to office.

"Lying to achieve a personal goal has almost reached the state of being a constitutional right. I intend to exercise my rights, along with the rest of my countrymen."

The prosecutor was incredulous, so he pleaded with the judge, "You can't allow this man to give testimony under oath. He as much as told you that he's going to lie on the stand."

The judge asked, "Mr. Ascenzio, do you plan to commit perjury?"

"No, Your Honor. I plan to tell the truth as I see it."

The prosecutor suggested to the judge, "Why don't you call a recess for the rest of the day? We have already passed the lunch hour, and that will give you the rest of the day to consider your decision. We can resume testimony in the morning when cooler heads will prevail."

"If I disallow this witness, I will have to declare a mistrial, which will have wasted everybody's time, and I'm not inclined to do that. I told both of you before the trial that once we started, the final arbitration would be in the hands of the jury. I'm going to allow his testimony and let the jurors decide if they believe him or not. If you don't like the outcome of his trial, Mr. Bauman, you always have the right to an appeal. Mr. Ascenzio, don't make a fool of me, or you'll regret it. Everybody, back in the courtroom."

When the cast of characters was reassembled in the courtroom, Judge Belowski did not give an explanation of her decision to the jurors or the gallery. She simply stated, "The defense will continue with its witness."

Carol Ann introduced the witness to those in the courtroom. "The witness is a gunnery sergeant in the United States Marine Corps. I have his permission to address him by his commonly accepted abbreviated title.

"Gunny, Detective Garlin has raised the possibility that there may be some hours missing in the defendant's description of his trip to see his parents in Florida. Can you shed any light on that issue?"

"Yes, he was with me."

"Gunny, please explain your time together."

"Earlier in the day of the trip, Jimmy called me and told me about his planned trip. I suggested that we get together before he left. We agreed to meet at my office in Quantico after he had dinner. We met and got caught up on the latest happenings in our lives. We reminisced about our corps experiences and our time in Iraq. I am thinking about retiring, so I asked a lot of questions about retirement and civilian life. In all, we spent a few hours together."

"Thank you, Gunny. I think your testimony accounts for the missing hours in the detective's calculation."

"Cross examine, Mr. Bauman?"

"Since you're in civilian clothes today, I'll refer to you as Mr. Ascenzio.

"Mr. Ascenzio, the defendant told detective Garlin that he started out on his trip to Florida after dinner. Was that statement accurate?"

"Yes, my office was on his route to Florida."

"Why do you think the defendant failed to tell the detective about the stopover with you?"

"Because it was none of the detective's damn business, and it didn't contradict the fact that the defendant started his trip after dinner."

"Would you lie to help a Marine buddy out of a jam?"

"Define a lie."

"Lie, as not the truth."

"Define truth."

"The opposite of a lie."

"Truth is relative, not absolute. One of the first things we learn in the Marine Corps is that your survival depends on the man next to you and his on you. A Marine will do anything necessary to make sure that other Marines survive. It's embedded in our souls and character. It is who we are and always will be."

"That's all I have for this witness."

"Redirect Miss Garnett?"

"No thank you, Your Honor. The witness has done his duty by appearing here today."

"In that case, we'll adjourn until tomorrow morning at 9:00."

Things did not go well for the prosecution because the defense had successfully countered most of the arguments presented by the DA, but if the jury was affronted by the gunny's testimony, then he might be able to snatch victory from defeat.

Carol Ann was determined not to lose this case, and to insure victory, she had a plan to send the trial sideways.

36

The Witness

Vince bolted out of the meeting on the day Jimmy was charged with murder and went in search of Nicky B. He remembered Nicky telling him about his mother's experiences in forensics.

Nicky's mother, Rosemarie nee Agosto, was a licensed physician with many years of experience in the field of forensics. Working at the CDC (Center for Disease Control) as a researcher, she assisted in the successful defense of a defendant accused of murder in Suffolk County, New York. She worked as a physician at the Veterans Administration hospital in Northport, New York. Most recently, her findings helped convict a murderer in Nassau County, New York. She used her maiden name professionally and her married name in personal matters.

Carol Ann knew of Rosemarie's accomplishments and enlisted her help in the Geracollo case. Together, they were able to obtain a federal court order that would allow Doctor Agosto to examine the paint scrapper found at the Pettite murder scene. The doctor used the MPD crime lab to conduct her investigation.

On the second morning of the trial, everyone was in place when Judge Belowski took her seat on the bench at 9:00 a.m.

Without delay, the judge ordered, "Miss Garnett, call your next witness."

"I call Doctor Rosemarie Agosto to the stand."

The DA was on his feet, "Objection! The witness is not on my witness list."

"What about that, Miss Garnett?"

"The name was not on the original list I sent to the prosecutor office, but a few days before the start of this trial, I called Mr.

Bauman's office and spoke to ADA Lawler. I instructed him to notify Mr. Bauman that I was adding the doctor to my witness list."

"I was never notified of the addition."

Judge Belowski countered, "You have a failure to communicate in your office, Mr. Bauman. I am going to let the doctor testify."

Before asking a question, Carol Ann addressed the judge and jury. "The doctor, by court order, examined a piece of evidence recovered from an earlier crime scene."

From the DA, "What crime scene?"

"The Nora Pettite murder," answered Carol Ann.

"Objection, Your Honor! What has that crime got to do with this case?"

The judge asked, "What have you got to say about that, Miss Garnett?"

"The doctor uncovered certain evidence on a paint scrapper that was not presented at the court-martial of the defendant. Had that evidence been presented at that trial, it would have completely exonerated Mr. Geracollo of the murder charge. In the interest of justice, I think the jury should consider that evidence when deciding a verdict at this trial."

"I'll allow the doctor to testify. I would like to hear what she has to say. Continue Miss Garnett."

"Doctor, what did your examination of the paint scrapper uncover?"

"My visual examination revealed some small porous holes between the scrapper's blade and handle. I separated the two parts and found blood and skin tissue samples. The blood belonged to the victim, Pettite, and the defendant. The tissue sample did not belong to either of them?"

"Were you able to identify the source of the skin samples?"

"Yes, I did DNA testing of the skin samples and identified the person who left the samples on the scrapper."

"Who was the person you identified?"

"Ensign Richard Settie."

The DA saw that the jury was awestruck, so he entreated the judge, "Please, Your Honor, you can't accept this testimony. It's irrelevant to this case."

"Mr. Bauman, you opened the door for the defense when you introduced the Settie testimony at the beginning of this trial. The defense is just following your lead. I'm going to allow the doctor's testimony. The defense may continue with the witness."

"That's all I have for this witness." Carol Ann thanked the doctor for her appearance and then took her seat.

"Cross examine, Mr. Bauman?"

"Doctor, do you think your testimony will excuse the defendant for the murder of Ensign Settie?"

"Objection!"

Judge Belowski cut off the defense counsel after the word "Objection," rapped her gavel, and said to the DA, "Sir, your question is completely out of order, and you know it."

"I'll withdraw the question."

"Now you may continue with your cross examination, but be very careful what you suggest. I'll not warn you again."

Bauman asked, "Did your evidence and conclusion prove that Mr. Settie murdered Nora Petite?"

"No."

"I'm finished with this witness."

"Call your next witness, Miss Garnett."

"The defense rests, Your Honor."

"We'll take a one hour recess, and then we'll have closing arguments."

After the break, Prosecutor Bauman led with a short closing argument. He stressed in various ways that the defendant was the only possible killer of Richard Settie.

Carol Ann also gave a short closing. She stressed that there was no conclusive evidence that connected the defendant to the murder of the victim.

The prosecutor was offered the last word, but he declined the opportunity to refute the defense's contention.

Judge Belowski gave her final instructions to the jury, informed the jurors that they would be served lunch during their deliberations, and then directed them to retire to the jury room and decide a verdict.

To the prosecution and the defense, she said, "Stay close to your phones. You'll be notified when the jury returns."

Carol Ann, Jimmy, and Vince waited in her office for the return of the jury. Three hours later, she got the call to return to the courtroom. The judge asked the jury foreman, "Madam Foreperson, has the jury reached a verdict?"

"No, Your Honor. We're deadlocked."

"I'm not going to accept that decision at this point." The judge then gave further instructions to the jurors and ordered them to continue deliberating.

Each side went their separate ways and waited for the next call. Just before 6:00 p.m., the call came.

Everyone was in place when the jury filed into the jury box. The judge asked again, "Madam Foreperson, has the jury reached a verdict?"

"No, Your Honor. We are hopelessly deadlocked. No one has changed their mind. We are split down the middle."

"Is there any possibility that you can reach a verdict if you continue to deliberate?"

"No, nobody is willing to change their position. This jury is as hung as hung can get."

The judge thanked the jurors and dismissed them. After the jurors filed out, the judge addressed the courtroom. "I'm going to declare a mistrial. Mr. Geracollo, I'd like to explain to you what happens next." Carol Ann and Jimmy stood, and the judge continued, "I'm going to dismiss the charges against you, but remember, the district attorney can recharge you at some time in the future. You are free to go."

The judge stood and said to the assembly, "Everyone have a nice day." She then left the courtroom.

Back in the jury room, one of the jurors said, "The press will want to talk to us. What should we do?"

There was a chorus of "No way", "Not me", "The press will screw up what we say," and other negative comments. One juror suggested, "Why don't we let Maria represent all of us. She likes to talk."

Maria agreed to be the spokesperson for the group, and when the press badgered the jurors outside the courthouse with questions, Maria stepped forward and stated, "I will meet with one representative of the press to discuss the case."

The press also questioned the DA, and one reporter asked, "Mr. Bauman, will you recharge the defendant?"

"I have not made that determination yet." The DA had no intention of recharging Jimmy. The trial had gone as well as he could have hoped for. He was never convinced, beyond the shadow of a doubt, that Jimmy killed Settie, and the introduction of the doctor's findings would get the Navy and the mayor off his back. He felt in a convoluted way that he had come out of the trial a winner.

Maria Greco met with the press representative at her home in mid-afternoon. The representative opened the interview with, "Can you describe what happened during the jury deliberation?"

"Confusion, shouting, doubt, and firm conviction."

"How was the jury divided?"

"Some of the jurors felt the DA had a good case because there were no other suspects for the murder, while others thought his case was weak when the defense started to poke holes in his witness's testimony."

"What did the jurors think of the Ascenzio testimony?"

"Again, division. Some thought it was an outright lie, and others thought it was plausible. Those with military experience sided with Ascenzio's contention that you do what you have to do to save a buddy if you believed he might not be innocent but was not guilty of murder if Settie killed Pettite. If that were the case, they believed the defendant was justified in killing Settie."

"How did the jury react to the doctor's testimony?"

"That testimony sent the deliberations into a tailspin. It didn't prove anything about the innocence of the defendant. It was probably harmful to the prosecution and helpful to the defense because it started the jurors thinking about things not related to the trial. In the minds of the jurors, it raised alternate theories of the defendant's conduct. It was a kind of left-handed jury nullification. After that testimony, everybody had their mind made up."

"What was the final verdict count?"

"Six for guilty, six for not guilty. It was set in stone. Years of deliberating would not have changed the final count."

The representative asked, "How did you vote?"

"That's none of your damn business."

Epilogue

Based on his testimony at the Geracollo court-martial, the Department of the Navy issued, posthumously, a Dishonorable Discharge for Ensign Richard Settie.

After the trial, Jimmy Geracollo proposed marriage to Carol Ann Garnett, and she accepted. Six months after the engagement, they married.

Vince Ascenzio retired from the Marine Corps and opened an import Italian food specialty business.

A few months after Vince's retirement, Commander Theresa Scafidi retired from the Navy.

Theresa and Vince decided to marry, and a year after their marriage, Theresa gave birth to a daughter. They named the child after Vince's father and called her Toni.

Nicky B is raising one of Lola's puppies. In keeping with tradition, he named the dog Lolita, Little Lola.

Doctor Rosemarie Agosto once more retired to the anonymity of private life.

Final Thoughts

If you ever find yourself in an argument with a Marine and the likelihood of violence against your person seems inevitable, you can protect yourself by saying to your tormentor, "You're crazy." Chances are he will agree with you, knowing that you have spoken a universal truth. In most cases, the disagreement will subside, and the two of you can go and enjoy a friendly drink.

We live in a dangerous world. If you want to feel safe, surround yourself with Marines.

CPSIA information can be obtained
at www.ICGtesting.com
Printed in the USA
FFOW01n1557240216
21794FF